"You've made me forget everything else.

"Was that what you wanted, to make me your fool?" Conrad looked at Laurel out of haunted eyes.

"If you're a fool, so am I," she said softly. "I forgot everything else, too."

He held her hands in a grip of iron. "If you're lying," he said hoarsely, "may you never be forgiven."

"Do you believe I'm lying?"

"God help me, I don't know."

"Why are you afraid of me?" she asked urgently.

"It's myself I fear, more than you. I thought I was safe, but you showed me I'm not. You bring magic with you, but it's the most dangerous magic in the world.... All my life, the Lorelei has haunted me. I knew I must confront her one day, but when the time came, I was taken by surprise."

Laurel ran her fingertips gently down his cheek and felt him tremble. "But why deny it?" she asked softly. "Suppose I *am* the Lorelei—what then?"

Dear Reader,

Though it may be cold outside during the month of November, it's always warmed by the promise of the upcoming holiday season. What better time to curl up with a good book? What better time for Silhouette Romance?

And in November, we've got some wonderful books to take the chill off these cold winter months. Continuing our DIAMOND JUBILEE celebration is *Song of the Lorelei*, by Lucy Gordon. Escape to the romantic world of brooding Conrad von Feldstein. The haunting secret at von Feldstein Castle is revealed when beautiful Laurel Blake pays a visit . . . and love finally comes home. Don't miss this emotional, poignant tale!

The DIAMOND JUBILEE—Silhouette Romance's tenth anniversary celebration—is our way of saying thanks to you, our readers. To symbolize the timelessness of love, as well as the modern gift of the tenth anniversary, we're presenting readers with a DIAMOND JUBILEE Silhouette Romance each month, penned by one of your favorite Silhouette Romance authors. And rounding up the year, next month be sure to watch for *Only the Nanny Knows for Sure*, by Phyllis Halldorson.

And that's not all! There are six books a month from Silhouette Romance—stories by wonderful writers who, time and time again, bring home the magic of love. During our anniversary year, each book is special and written with romance in mind. This month, and in the future, work by such loved writers as Diana Palmer, Brittany Young and Annette Broadrick is sure to put a smile on your face.

During our tenth anniversary, the spirit of celebration is with us year-round. And that's all due to you, our readers. With the support you've given to us, you can look forward to many more years of heartwarming, poignant love stories.

I hope you'll enjoy this book and all of the stories to come. Come home to romance—Silhouette Romance—for always!

Sincerely,
Tara Hughes Gavin
Senior Editor

LUCY GORDON

Song of
the Lorelei

Published by Silhouette Books New York

America's Publisher of Contemporary Romance

SILHOUETTE BOOKS
300 E. 42nd St., New York, N.Y. 10017

ISBN: 0-373-08754-3

First Silhouette Books printing November 1990

LUCY GORDON

met her husband-to-be in Venice, fell in love the first evening and got engaged two days later. After seventeen years they're still happily married and now live in England with their three dogs. For twelve years Lucy was a writer on an English women's magazine. She interviewed many of the world's most interesting men, including Warren Beatty, Richard Chamberlain, Roger Moore, Sir Alec Guinness and Sir John Gielgud.

In 1985 she won the *Romantic Times* Reviewers Choice Award for Outstanding Series Romance Author. She has also won a Golden Leaf Award from the New Jersey Chapter of the RWA and was a finalist in the RWA Golden Medallion contest for her Silhouette Romance, *A Pearl Beyond Price*.

Dear Readers,

Sometimes it hardly seems like seven years since I wrote
my first romance for Silhouette. At other times, it seems
like a whole era has passed, because my life is now filled
with so many new people. There are the friends I've made
at Silhouette Books itself, and the friendships I've formed
through the mail when readers were kind enough to write
to me.

And then there are the people I've met in my books, who
are often as unpredictable to me as anyone in real life. I
start with the outline of a plot, but the details come as I
write, and often characters will tap me on the arm and tell
me I've got them all wrong.

While learning about them, I've learned about myself. I
never knew I had a fascination with the kind of man who
feels more than he can say until I realized he was edging his
way into my books too often to be a coincidence. You'll
meet him in *The Song of the Lorelei*. And in my next book
for Silhouette, a Desire, you'll find my other favorite hero:
the brooding, volcanic Italian.

When I started writing romances, the male point of view
was very rare. It is much more common now because you,
the readers, have shown that you enjoy it. The other big
difference in romances is the way I think they have helped
women to see themselves in a better light, as strong,
capable, and proud. We've become resolute in what we
expect from men—and what we let them get away with. I
believe romances partly reflect this, and partly explain it.

But their real secret lies in what *doesn't* change: the
timeless magic that appears without warning between a
man and a woman. As long as we have that magic to hope
for, dream about, or remember, we will never lose the
secret of life.

Best wishes,
Lucy Gordon

Chapter One

As the boat rounded a bend of the Rhine, Laurel leaned forward eagerly against the rail, catching her first glimpse of the Lorelei rock. It towered four hundred feet above the river, looking stern and forbidding in its austere grandeur. She took an excited breath as she finally saw the place she had dreamed about for so long.

High up on the opposite bank rose Feldstein Castle, its towers and turrets seeming to grow directly out of the surrounding trees. It, too, held a magical attraction for her, and unconsciously she slipped her hand into her purse and touched the little packet.

A plump woman came to stand beside her. "So that's the Lorelei rock," she said breathlessly. "It looks really scary, doesn't it?"

"I don't know about scary," Laurel said contemplatively. "It's certainly majestic."

"Oh, I think it's scary. I can just see the beautiful maiden sitting high up there, singing her mournful song, and the sailor listening so hard that he was lured onto the rocks, and drowned."

Laurel smiled. "You like your legends tragic."

"The more tragic, the better," the woman confirmed cheerfully. She peered down. "I can't see any rocks."

"There are seven of them far below, and they're called the Seven Virgins. They're supposed to have been beautiful women who swore never to marry, and turned themselves to stone to avoid their suitors. Now they lie in wait for the unwary sailor, and the Lorelei sings to draw their victims in."

The woman shivered pleasurably. "How lovely. My name's Clarice, by the way."

"Mine's Laurel."

"Laurel! Just like the Lorelei!"

"Yes. My grandmother came from Hargen, that little town over there, just below Feldstein Castle. She made my parents call me Laurel. She raised me after they died, and told me wonderful tales of the Rhine and its legends. But the legend of the Lorelei was always our favorite."

"Is she with you on this trip?"

"No." Laurel's face clouded. "She died last month, but she wanted me to come back to her birthplace, and I promised her that I would." Once again she touched the packet inside her purse.

"And you're really doing it. That's lovely."

Laurel smiled fondly. "She was very strong-willed. I got used to doing what she wanted."

The words were inadequate to describe Anna, a powerful personality who'd seemed sure to live for-

ever, but who'd died suddenly of pneumonia. Laurel
had known not only grief but a profound sense of
shock that the woman who had been her only family
for most of her twenty-four years was no longer there
in the flesh. She could, however, still feel her influence. Anna had left her a small painting of the Rhine
gorge at sunset, along with a letter advising her to sell
it.

"It might be worth a couple of thousand pounds,"
Anna had written. "I only wish it could be more."

To Laurel's amazement, the first dealer she'd con-
sulted offered her one hundred thousand pounds for
the picture. "It's actually one of a pair," he told her,
"and if you had the other one they'd be worth a million together."

Laurel had taken the picture home and put it away
carefully to give herself time to think. Before she
rushed into a decision, she had a promise to keep.

Anna's other legacy had been a small, sealed packet.
"Go to Feldstein Castle," she'd said just before she
died, "and give this to Baron Kaspar von Feldstein. He
will understand." Her thin, lined face had broken into
a smile of sudden radiance, as she added, "He loved
me once."

"But Gran," Laurel had said gently, "suppose he
isn't alive now?"

"He is alive. And his wife died last year or I would
not ask you to do this. Oh yes," she nodded at Laurel's look of surprise, "I know a great deal about him.
I knew his wedding day, although he did not know
mine." Her face was shadowed. "I knew the day his
son was born, and his grandson, too. And I know he is
alive, because if he were not I would have felt it *here*."
She laid a hand over her breast. "But since you are

young and haven't yet discovered the great power of love, I will give you more practical evidence.''

She'd produced a page torn from a magazine. A picture showed an old man against a background of huge barrels, and the caption read, *Baron Kaspar von Feldstein receives a consignment of local wine to be turned into brandy at the famous Feldstein distillery.* It was dated a few weeks earlier.

Laurel had looked at the tall man, still handsome and impressive despite his age, and known that this was the answer to a mystery that had puzzled her for years. Anna had sometimes spoken to her of a man she'd loved in her youth, and there'd been a note of vibrant passion in her voice that made her granddaughter look at her with wonder. It was as though she'd once had a vision so brilliant and beautiful that the years had had no power to dim its force, a vision that had illuminated her whole life.

Laurel's own youthful romances had been colored by the reflected light of Anna's vision. She was never tempted to read too much into flirtation, because she lived with a woman who'd known a great love and been touched by it forever. It was impossible to imagine any of the commonplace young men she dated haunting her forever, and the instinctive comparison built a barrier around her heart. The man who would evoke her love would have to be of the same mettle as Anna's unknown lover.

She'd thought of him as ''unknown'' because although she'd learned a great deal about him, Anna had kept his name locked in her heart. Until now.

''This is him, isn't it?'' she said. ''The man you've told me about.''

Anna smiled. "Yes, that is him. Ah, if you could only have seen him when I knew him, how splendid he was, how strong and beautiful." She became young again as her eyes glowed with happy remembrance. "And he loved *me*. I was his first love, and he was mine."

"Why didn't you marry him, Gran?"

The look of youthfulness faded abruptly from Anna's face, leaving her tired and ill again. "You make it all sound so simple. A boy and girl fall in love, and they marry. To your generation it *is* simple. You ignore the barriers that we believed were insuperable, and it is wise of you to do so. If I had it to do again, I know I should act differently. But I was a daughter of my time. I obeyed the rules. And so I broke his heart—and my own." She sighed and pushed the package into Laurel's hands. "Go to him, *liebchen*," she pleaded. "Promise that you will do this for me. It matters so much."

And Laurel had said, "Gran, I promise. I'll find him. I'll make sure he gets your message."

Anna had smiled wearily. "Then I can rest." She'd closed her eyes.

Laurel had buried her grandmother a few days later.

Among her things she'd found a lock of hair. It was russet-colored and still shone as it must have the day Anna had cut it from her lover's head. There was also a photograph of a young man and woman clothed in fashions of nearly sixty years ago. He was a much younger version of the man in the magazine picture, tall, marvellously good-looking, with a lean, serious face and a proud demeanor. The young woman had long, gleaming fair hair that flowed over her shoulders, almost to her waist, and she leaned against him so that his arm around her caressed her tresses. Their joy in each other was so great that they hardly seemed aware of the camera.

The picture had saddened Laurel. The two young people had been so happy, so cocooned in their love, yet it had all come to nothing. They had separated. Anna had married an Englishman and gone to live in his country, never to see her homeland again. The streaming golden hair that Kaspar had loved had been cut short and pinned severely back, and the years had thinned it and turned it gray. But the gold had reappeared in her granddaughter. Laurel, too, wore her fair hair long, and was as proud of her crowning glory as Anna had once been of hers.

Her fluent German meant she was much in demand as a translator. She worked free-lance and could arrange time off to make the trip she'd promised. Instead of flying, she booked a Rhine cruise so that she could see some of the great river, whose legends had always filled her dreams. She chose the cheapest one because she hadn't grown used to the idea that she was worth a possible hundred thousand pounds.

And now here she was within sight of her goal. As the boat docked at Hargen, Laurel prepared to make her way up to the castle. No one knew she was coming. She'd tried to write to the baron, but the right words wouldn't come. She'd decided that she must speak to him personally.

Laurel discovered that Hargen was a picture-book village, full of winding cobbled streets and half-timbered houses. Where the walls weren't timbered, some of the houses had elaborate pictures painted on their exteriors. Baskets of flowers hung from every window and wherever she looked, Laurel saw cheerfulness and impeccable order.

The village was built on a slope. Laurel had decided to walk to her destination. She followed the streets upward, in the direction of the castle. Gradually the village fell away, and she was left with a steep road that led up between trees. After ten minutes climbing without seeming to make much progress, she began to wish she'd taken a taxi. But it was too late now, and she continued onward and upward until she arrived, breathless, at a huge pair of wrought iron gates that were firmly locked.

She rang, and after a moment an elderly man appeared from inside the gatehouse. "Yes?" he asked suspiciously.

"I'd like to see the baron," Laurel said pleasantly. "Will you please let me in?"

"Nobody can see the baron. You ought to know that. What's your business?"

"It's private. I must see him."

"Private, is it? You can do better than that. The last journalist who tried to get in here was more ingenious. Be off with you."

"I'm not a journalist," Laurel started to say, but the man had already turned back into the gatehouse. A moment later, two vicious looking Dobermans streaked out and hurled themselves at the gate, barking furiously. Startled, she backed away and began to skirt the boundary wall, the old man's self-satisfied chuckle ringing in her ears.

It had never occurred to Laurel that she'd be turned away. Now she wasn't sure what to do. The wall was ten feet high. The row of spikes, which studded the top was evidence of a great determination to keep out the world. Why had she been mistaken for a journalist? And why was no one allowed to see the baron?

She walked around the wall for a long time, without finding a chink in the defenses. She passed two gates, but they were solid oak and bolted firmly.

She was close to despair when instead of solid brick she found bars that started three feet up and rose to the top. Beyond them was a garden, exquisitely groomed and manicured. No weed would have dared show its head. No blade of grass would have been so presumptuous as to grow a fraction of an inch longer than the others. In the center, disconsolately bouncing a ball by himself, was a little boy of about ten.

He looked up, and his face brightened when he saw her. Quickly he ran over to the bars. He had a pleasant, open face with dark brown eyes and a delightful smile. "Hello," he said in German.

"Hello. You look very dismal by yourself."

"I'm always by myself. There's no one to talk to."

"Can't you have some of your school friends here?"

"I don't have any. Uncle Conrad won't let me go to school. He won't let me do anything. He won't even let me be in the carnival procession, and I'm old enough, too."

"He sounds like a terrible fusspot," Laurel said sympathetically.

"He is. And now he says I can't see my grandfather. He's really my *great*-grandfather, but I call him Grandpa because Great-grandpa takes too long. He isn't well, but I just know he'd feel better if I was there."

"Do you mean the old baron?" Laurel asked with a twinge of alarm.

"That's right. Do you know him?"

"I've heard of him. Look, do you think you could let me in somehow?"

"There's a gate just along there. I can get the key. I'm not supposed to know where it is, but I do." He raced away.

Laurel looked around anxiously. She was suddenly aware of the urgency of the situation. Somehow she must get to the baron while there was still time to deliver Anna's message.

In a few moments, the boy returned with the key and unlocked a pair of wrought iron gates, which opened into the garden. "Are we going to play a game?" he asked eagerly.

"Later perhaps. First I want you to tell me where Grandpa is."

"It's no use. Uncle Conrad has told the nurses to let no one up to his room in the tower unless he gives permission."

"I'll manage somehow. Which way is the tower?"

He took her hand. "I'll show you."

He led her into the castle by a side door, up a flight of stairs, then down a corridor, and another, and another, until Laurel lost count. At last she found herself in a large, circular room. A desk dominated the center, and around it were several leather chairs, which looked old and comfortable. There were some massive bookshelves, a few pictures and a huge tapestry hanging on the wall. "This is Grandpa's room," the little boy explained. "That door over there leads to the stairway to his bedroom, which is just above us."

Laurel looked at the massive oak door with its iron fittings. It looked forbidding, and for a moment she hesitated. Was she doing the right thing bursting in on a sick old man? It might be best to find out a little about his illness first. "I don't know your name," she said to the child.

"I'm Horst von Feldstein," he said with a charming, old-fashioned little bow.

"I'm Laurel Blake."

"Were you called Laurel because you look like the Lorelei?"

"I don't think so. Anyway, no one knows exactly what she looked like."

"I do. She had long golden hair like yours, and she sat on the rock combing it with a golden comb while she sang. You can see it in the picture. Look."

He ran over to the tapestry and pulled it aside to reveal a door. Once he had managed to push it open, Laurel followed him, finding herself in a small anteroom, almost bare except for a large picture on the far wall. It was a painting of a beautiful young woman looking down into the waters of the Rhine. Her blonde tresses streamed to her waist, and with one hand she let them flow through her fingers, emphasizing their sensuous beauty to the shadowy figure of the sailor below. Her face bore an elusive half-smile, as if she were exulting in her power to lure a man to destruction. Laurel drew in her breath, for the painting was a masterpiece, capturing the timeless mystery and danger of the legend.

"You see—it's you," Horst insisted. "You look just like her."

A sound made them both look around quickly. Framed in the doorway stood the angriest man Laurel had ever seen. He was in his early thirties, tall, with russet-brown hair and dark eyes framed by a lean face. He had a firm, generous mouth that might have been attractive if it hadn't been pulled into a hard, angry line. "I take it you're the young woman who tried to get past the gatekeeper," he said. "Luckily he warned me. How did you get in?"

Laurel didn't answer, not wanting to get Horst into trouble. The man walked over to her and stood looking down the several inches that separated them. Guessing it was his intention to intimidate her, she raised her chin. "I asked you a question and I expect to have it answered at once," he barked.

"It was me, Uncle Conrad," Horst said in a faint voice. "I opened the gate."

"It wasn't his fault," Laurel said quickly. "I persuaded him."

"That, I can well believe. Is there nothing your kind won't stoop to?"

"I don't know what you mean by 'my kind'—"

"Save your breath. You know very well what I mean."

"The gatekeeper thought I was a journalist, but I'm not. I'd have told him so if he hadn't let the dogs out."

"Those dogs are there to deter interlopers, which they do very efficiently."

"I'm not an interloper," Laurel said indignantly. "I'm a respectable visitor and I urgently need to see the baron."

Conrad's wry smile only just escaped being a sneer. "So I've heard. Private business, but you can't say what it is."

"Only to the baron himself. You *must* let me see him."

"Young woman, nobody tells me what I must do—"

"I didn't mean— Look, it's urgent. I have something to give him, something I promised to deliver."

"You can give it to me."

"Oh no," she said, taking a step backward. Nothing on earth would persuade her to hand over the precious package to this stern, cold-eyed man. "I have to place it in the baron's own hands."

Her stubbornness made his face tighten with even more anger. Suddenly he moved forward, forcing her to retreat a step, then another, until he had backed her out of the anteroom. "I'll tell you one more time, you're not going to see him. What you are going to do is leave, *now*." He picked up a telephone on the desk, dialed a single figure, and barked into it, "Have my car brought around to the front right away." He slammed down the receiver and turned back to Laurel. "Where are you staying?"

"Why should that matter?"

"It matters because I'm taking you there to make sure you collect your things and then leave this district."

"I'm not staying anywhere. I'm on a cruise."

"Which boat?"

"I don't see—"

"Which boat?"

"The *Bergen*."

"Right. Then we'll go there immediately."

He clasped his hand around her arm in a grip that allowed no refusal. Laurel tried to jerk away, but found herself being hurried out of the room so fast that her feet barely touched the ground. "Let go of me," she snapped.

"I'm taking no chances," he said grimly.

"You must be quite mad to think you can treat people like this."

"It's how I treat trespassers and people who are up to no good."

"You don't even *know* what I'm up to," she said, breathless from the rapid pace.

"I know you're very vague about explaining yourself, and that's suspicious enough for me."

Furious at his high-handedness, Laurel managed to grab a doorjamb as they passed. The sudden check surprised him enough for her to wriggle free of his grasp, but she managed to run only a few steps before he caught her. "All right, if you want to play the hard way," he said grimly, and swung her up into his arms. Laurel found herself held tightly against a broad, muscular chest whose heat penetrated her thin dress and communicated directly with her body. She had no choice but to hold onto his shoulder with one hand while the other automatically pushed against him, but to no avail. His arms were like steel bands around her, holding her so tightly against him that she could feel the soft thunder of his heart. It was beating fast, and so was her own.

Her breath caught in her throat and she couldn't trust herself to speak. Her head was spinning, and her whole view was taken up by the closeness of his firm chin and wide, sensual mouth.

Abruptly he stopped and put her down. For the last few yards she'd been so totally aware of this man that she hadn't noticed her surroundings. Now she saw that they were outside the castle and his car was waiting, just as he'd commanded. "Get in," he said tersely, holding open the passenger door.

Furiously, she did as she was told. He climbed into the driver's seat and pressed a button, causing all four doors to lock. "So you won't jump out," he explained.

He started the engine and drove to the iron gates, which now stood open. The gatekeeper was there with the two dogs on leashes. Conrad stopped and called out to him, "Take a good look at her, Boris, and memorize her face. If she tries to get in again, detain her and call the police."

He drove to the river with Laurel sitting beside him, seething with suppressed anger. At last he pulled up by the pier, saying, "If you're entertaining the idea of slipping off the boat when my back is turned, let me tell you that there are only two small hotels in Hargen, neither of which will offer you a room. You can take my word for it."

"Perhaps they won't fall over themselves to do your bidding," Laurel said spiritedly.

He smiled coldly. "It wouldn't be wise to gamble on that. You would find yourself sleeping in the streets and arrested as a vagrant."

"I don't believe this is happening," she snapped. "What are you? Some kind of feudal dictator?"

Without answering, he unlocked the door. "You can go now."

"Look, if you'd only listen for a moment—"

Conrad got out of the car and came around to her side, opening the door and taking her arm. "Out," he ordered.

Laurel climbed out, and he stood looking down at her. "Let me make it clear that under no circumstances are you to return to Feldstein Castle," he said coldly. "Remember my words, or I promise you, you'll be very sorry."

Without waiting for an answer, he returned to the car and drove off. She watched him go, silently calling him all the worst names she could think of.

She had no doubt that he was as powerful as he claimed. Conrad von Feldstein radiated a personal force that was almost tangible. How could she complete her mission with that intractable man set against her? And yet, to delay it might mean that she wouldn't reach the baron in time.

She boarded the boat and went to the cafeteria, where she bought herself a cup of coffee and sat brooding while it got cold. The one thing she wasn't going to do was give up. The memory of Anna's pleading voice whispering, "Promise me, *liebchen*..." ensured that, and so did her own fighting spirit. But storming the castle was out of the question. She would have to use guile, slipping back when Conrad thought her safely out of the way.

The swaying of the boat told her they were starting up, and Laurel went on deck. As she had half expected, Conrad had returned and was watching the boat's departure. He saw her and raised his hand in an ironic salute, which annoyed her even more. She stayed where she was, and saw that he didn't move until he was sure she'd been safely dispatched.

Clarice appeared and buttonholed her for a session of gossip. It was the last thing Laurel wanted, but she endured it for half an hour before escaping on the pretext of getting ready for supper. She let herself into her cabin and sat down on the bed, feeling dejected.

Suddenly, an unfamiliar noise made her look up. There was no one else in the cabin, yet she had the strange sensation that she was not alone. She heard the noise again, and this time she could tell that it came from the wardrobe. Quickly, she pulled open the door. She stared in disbelief.

"Horst!" she exclaimed. "What are you doing here?"

"I've run away," said the little boy, stepping out of the wardrobe. He looked up at her stubbornly. "I don't like it at home. I want to stay with you."

She sat down on the bed. "How on earth did you get out?"

"Through the back gate, the one where I let you in. And then I locked it behind me and threw the key into the bushes so that no one would guess for ages. I ran to the river as fast as I could, and slipped onto the boat when no one was looking."

"How did you get into my cabin?"

"I told one of the stewards that I was with you and I'd got locked out, so he let me in. Wasn't I clever?"

"I wonder if your uncle will be impressed with your cleverness," Laurel said wryly.

"I don't care. I'm never going back to Uncle Conrad. He won't let me be in the carnival procession, and it's not *fair*. Don't send me back, Lorelei, *please*. It's horrible. There's no one to play with there, and nothing to do."

Her mind was in turmoil. She pitied the child, imprisoned in that gloomy building, in the care of a man who seemed to be made of stone. But there was no doubt as to what she must do. "Horst, I'm sorry," she said. "But I have to send you back."

"No." He flung his arms around her neck. "Please—I hate it there."

She held him soothingly, but insisted, "Horst, you must go back. There isn't any choice. Come on, dry your eyes. We'd better go and see the Captain."

He sniffed but obeyed her. When she had dried his face she led him outside and up the little flight of stairs that led to the main deck. At once, she became aware that people were leaning over the side of the boat, exclaiming with excitement at some activity below. She looked over, and her heart almost stopped.

The Bergen was halting to let a police launch pull alongside it. It was manned by three burly-looking policemen, and standing with them, his face black with fury, was Conrad.

A metal staircase was lowered, and a policeman hurried up onto the deck of the *Bergen*. Conrad was close behind, and Laurel saw him point to her. At once, the policeman pushed his way through the crowd until he reached her. "You are Fräulein Blake?" he demanded.

"Yes, but—"

"You are under arrest."

"On what charge?" she gasped.

"Kidnapping this child. Herr von Feldstein, do you identify this woman as the intruder you discovered in the castle?"

"I do," Conrad said grimly.

"Fräulein, you will please come with me at once."

"No—wait—there's been a mistake."

"You can tell us about it at the station," he said, reaching for her arm.

Wildly, Laurel fended him off, but she felt as though she was in a nightmare and had weights on her limbs.

She heard Horst crying, "Leave my friend alone."

Then the little boy thrust himself between them. The movement threw her off balance, and suddenly there was nothing under her feet. She grabbed frantically at the wall, but it was too late, and she went tumbling down the stairs. A blazing shaft of pain went through her ankle, and something struck her head. There were shouts, people hanging over her, Horst crying miserably, "Lorelei . . . Lorelei. . . ."

Then, she blacked out.

Chapter Two

Laurel was in darkness, her only reality a throbbing ankle and a headache. She floated somewhere a long way below the surface of life, in a world full of echoes. It was quite pleasant, but she couldn't give in to it, because something was knocking on the door of her conscience... something she hadn't done... a promise to keep... and there wasn't much time....

A faint touch on her cheek brought her reluctantly back to reality. She forced herself to open her eyes, and then realized she must still be dreaming, because Conrad von Feldstein was there, leaning over her and brushing a strand of hair back from her eyes.

It was incredible that this harsh man could be so gentle, yet the sensation of his fingertips against her skin was feather-light. His expression, too, was different. Instead of anger, there was almost a look of bewilderment as he studied her face, and he had a haggard appearance, as though he needed sleep.

Then he became aware of her gaze and snatched his hand back, coloring slightly. His manner grew tense and aloof, as if he'd retreated to a place deep within himself. "I'm glad you are awake, Fräulein," he said politely. "How do you feel?"

"Like someone who fell down a flight of stairs," she said, fighting for lucidness. "Where am I?"

"In the hospital in Hargen."

She turned her head slightly and saw that she was in a pleasant little room with large windows. Outside, the sun was shining, but the blinds had been pulled, throwing the room into mellow shadow. "How long have I been here?"

"Since yesterday."

"What's the matter with me?"

"I'm afraid your ankle is broken, and you received a nasty knock on the head. I had you carried off the boat and brought here."

"I didn't kidnap Horst," she said suddenly.

"I know you didn't. He has told me everything that happened." He took a deep breath and spoke his next words with difficulty. "Please accept my apology for wrongly accusing you to the police, and accidentally causing you an injury."

Laurel managed a faint smile. "It half killed you to say that, didn't it?" she asked.

"I'm not used to apologizing," Conrad agreed, "but I believe in doing my duty." Unexpectedly, a faint smile touched his lips, "Besides, I have to put things right with Horst. He's very angry with me for 'being horrible' to you, as he put it. But you must admit that your behavior was suspicious."

"I don't admit anything of the kind."

"Well, we'll have time to argue about that when I've taken you home."

"Home?"

"You will complete your recovery in the castle. I'll take you there as soon as the doctor says it's safe."

"Indeed?" She felt nettled at this high-handedness.

"You have no choice. The *Bergen* has sailed. The Captain told me you came from England, so you're stranded in a strange country. You must stay at my home until you are well."

"My things—"

"Naturally, I had them all removed from the boat."

"And naturally everyone did as you told them?"

"They usually do," he said, sounding surprised. "Why not?"

"I can't think of a single reason why not," she agreed ironically. Suddenly, a dreadful thought struck her. "My purse, where is it?"

"Here." He handed it to her and she opened it quickly, sliding her hand inside until her fingers located the precious package. The look of relief on her face made Conrad's lips tighten. "You must have a very poor opinion of me, Fräulein," he said coldly. "I'm not a thief."

"I'm sorry— I didn't mean—"

"On the contrary, you meant exactly that. Why deny it?"

"Well, can you blame me? You made your position very plain. After the way you threw me out, I can't imagine why you would want me in your home."

"I don't want you," he said with sudden vehemence. "But it is my duty. Nothing more. And let me repeat my position so that it remains plain. You will not be allowed to see the baron under any circumstances whatsoever. I've taken steps to ensure that you don't get near him. I'll go now, but before I do—'' he paused, and his manner softened. ''If you can bear it, I'd like Horst to see you for a moment, just to reassure him.''

''Of course.''

Conrad looked out into the corridor, and a moment later Horst came hurrying in. His face was tearful. ''Only a moment,'' Conrad told him. ''Fräulein Blake is very tired.''

''But she isn't Fräulein Blake,'' Horst protested. ''She's the Lorelei.'' Looking over his head, Laurel was puzzled to see Conrad's mouth tighten. ''I'm sorry you got hurt because of me,'' Horst said.

''I'm fine,'' she told him firmly, although her head ached.

Horst was looking at her arm where the imprint of Conrad's fingers had left faint but perceptible bruises. ''Did you get those falling down the stairs?'' he asked.

Conrad's face filled with tension. Laurel bit back the truth. ''No, that was another accident,'' she said lamely.

''You have lots of accidents, don't you?'' Horst inquired innocently.

''That's enough, Horst,'' Conrad interrupted. ''Say goodbye now.''

''Goodbye. But I'll see you again, won't I? Uncle Conrad says you're coming home with us soon.''

He'd told Horst before even asking her, Laurel noted wryly. But she only said, ''That's right.''

''Horst, go back to your mother now,'' Conrad ordered, watching Laurel's face.

When the child had gone, he said, ''Thank you. That was generous of you.'' He took her arm in his large, gentle hand and studied the bruises. His mouth had a twist of self-condemnation. "I'm sorry I hurt you. I didn't know I'd held you so hard. The fact is, when I lose my temper I sometimes don't realize what I'm doing. Horst wouldn't have understood—"

"It's your fault he ran away," Laurel said, clinging to logical thought while she could still manage it. "You smother him."

Conrad drew in a breath, and his face was as hard as it had been when she had first seen him. "My car will come for you as soon as you are well enough to travel," he said.

Laurel reflected that it would be a pleasure to take him down a peg with a firm refusal to accommodate his wishes. What restrained her was the realization that against all odds she'd managed to get into the castle.

"Good day," he said, and left abruptly.

Then, for no apparent reason, she had a shockingly clear memory of being carried in his arms, pressed against the firm muscles of his chest, breathing in the clean, spicy smell of his body. A surge of warmth passed through her.

Horst visited her again the next day, accompanied by a woman in her early thirties with a thin face and an anxious air. She was dressed expensively, but with little sense of style. She introduced herself as Johanna, Horst's mother. "My son insisted on coming to see you," she said. "You are his great friend."

"I'm sorry about his running away," Laurel said. "I didn't encourage him."

"I don't blame you. He's a rascal," Johanna said, looking dotingly at her son, who wriggled uncomfortably in the timeless manner of little boys. "I'm very

glad you're coming to stay with us," Johanna continued. "It will be nice for me to have a woman to talk to
amidst all those men."

"*All* those men?" Laurel queried.

"My husband, Markus, was the second of three
brothers. He died five years ago, and now I live with
my brothers-in-law and their grandfather, the old
baron. He's a dear old man, and Horst is the apple of
his eye." She reached out to caress her son, but he
managed to escape.

Before Laurel could ask about the baron, the door
opened and a young man breezed into the room. His
hair was the same russet color as Conrad's, and his face
bore just enough resemblance to stamp them as
brothers. But Conrad was a man. This was little more
than an attractive boy, with a boy's merry eyes and
carefree manner.

"This is my brother-in-law, Friederich," Johanna
said, smiling. "Friederich, this is Fräulein Blake."

"Please, call me Laurel," she said, addressing them
both.

"It will be a pleasure," Friederich said, taking her
hand and giving her a little bow.

"I didn't know you were coming here," Johanna
said.

Friederich greeted her with a peck on the cheek and
said, "I came to pay my respects to the Lorelei. After
last night's little scene, I was intrigued to discover what
all the fuss was about."

"What little scene?" Laurel asked.

"Conrad was annoyed with Horst for calling you the
Lorelei. I don't know why. I think it suits you very well.
I can just imagine you singing your sweet song and

luring helpless men to their doom. I swear I'm your slave already.''

Laurel laughed at his droll expression. There was something instantly likable about Friederich. ''When can you leave the hospital?'' he asked.

''The doctor says I'll be ready tomorrow.''

''Splendid. I'll bring the car myself.''

The next afternoon Friederich arrived and wheeled her out to the hospital entrance. He was driving a convertible with the top down. ''I thought you'd find this car easier to get into,'' he explained, helping her out of the wheelchair. ''Now, put your arms around my neck.''

She did so and felt him lift her up and deposit her gently in the back seat of the car. He held her easily, but Laurel had a sense that something was missing. There was no excitement in Friederich's arms, no sense of latent power. His mouth was handsome, but its closeness carried no hint of danger. Then she realized that her thoughts had drifted to Conrad, and she felt suddenly self-conscious.

Boris, the gatekeeper, stared as he saw her being driven through the main gates in style. Laurel couldn't resist giving him a cheery wave as she sailed past.

Friederich grinned. ''I gather you two have met before,'' he said.

''He thought I was a journalist and called the dogs out. He spoke as though you'd been plagued by journalists.''

''Yes, my grandfather is a prominent man in this area. The brandy distillery isn't large, but it's among the finest in the world. He achieved that single-handedly by insisting on quality and refusing to be too commercial. When he had a heart attack recently, the press started running stories about 'the end of an era'. Some of them have tried to worm their way in to get 'the last interview'.''

Laurel would have liked to ask more, but she didn't want to arouse Friederich's suspicions, and they'd almost reached the end of the winding driveway. Now she could see the true magnificence of the castle.

It was constructed of gray stone and stood proudly on the crest of the hill, with towers that seemed to rear up into the sky. It was a fairy-tale castle, a place of mystery where the most romantic legends could become reality. A shiver went down Laurel's spine.

Horst came bounding through the great oak front door to meet her, followed closely by Johanna. Friederich helped Laurel into the wheelchair and took her inside, escorted by Johanna and Horst.

''I hope you will like your bedroom,'' Johanna said. ''You're on the ground floor, so you'll have no trouble with stairs.''

Laurel gasped when she looked out her window, which overlooked the gorge. Four hundred feet below, the Rhine glittered and flashed in the afternoon sun, and she was sure she had never seen such beauty.

''You can see the Lorelei rock over there,'' Horst said, pointing across the river.

''That's enough, Horst,'' Johanna said quickly. ''Your uncle said not to talk like that.''

Horst looked as if he'd like to argue, but at that moment a middle-aged woman in a nurse's uniform bustled in.

''This is Helga,'' Johanna explained. ''I'm sure she wants to talk to you, so we'll leave you alone.'' Firmly, she shepherded the others out of the room.

"I'm going to put you straight to bed," Helga said. "Because of your head injury, you must rest a great deal over the next few days."

"I do feel a little tired, even after that short journey," Laurel admitted. She let Helga help her into the big bed, and lay back luxuriously.

"I'll come back when you've had some sleep," Helga promised.

Laurel dozed off almost at once, and awoke several hours later to find it was early evening and Helga had returned with her supper. She yawned and stretched, announcing that she was feeling better.

"Good," the nurse said briskly. "You'll soon be ready to spend more time out of bed, and we can decide on your routine."

"Do I need a routine?"

"Every sickroom needs a routine," Helga said firmly. "I insist on it—or at least, I try to."

Her tone hinted at a battle recently lost and Laurel asked, "But you don't always succeed?"

"I'm really here to nurse the baron. There's a spare room near him, and I did suggest that it would be more efficient for me if you were put there, but Herr von Feldstein wouldn't hear of it. He insisted that you must be down here. It's very inefficient."

Conrad might simply have put her on the ground floor to save her from having difficulty with the stairs, but Laurel was convinced he was keeping her as far from the baron as possible. "I heard the baron had suffered a heart attack," she said, trying not to sound too interested.

"Yes, a month ago."

"A month," Laurel mused. "You don't know exactly when, do you?"

"It was on the 15th. Why?"

"Nothing, I was just curious." A sudden eerie feeling suffused her. She felt as if she'd caught a glimpse of another world. Anna had died on the 15th.

"It was a massive attack, and it seemed he would surely die," Helga remembered. "But he hung on and managed to stabilize. Now he gets no better and no worse. It's almost as though he's ready to go, but something is holding him back." She shrugged and left the room.

Laurel finished her supper and lay back on her pillows. Her bed was near the window, and through it she could look directly across at the Lorelei rock. The setting sun had gilded it and it seemed to float in the distance, aloof and magical.

It might only be coincidence that the baron had collapsed on the day Anna died, but her heart whispered that there was more to it than that. The nurse had suspected the truth without understanding it.

Something was holding him back. He was waiting, and in this place of romantic legends and mystery, it was easy to believe that he was waiting for Laurel herself—and the message from the woman he had once loved.

She spent the first few days quietly, sleeping a good deal of the time. Horst seized every excuse to slip into her room, but Johanna never let him stay for long.

Then, one morning Laurel awoke to find herself feeling alert and normal again. Helga helped her dress and brought out the wheelchair. "You'll need this for a while," she said. "Then you can try crutches."

Friederich wheeled her into a large, sunny room where a table was set for breakfast. Johanna and Conrad were already seated, but Conrad rose courteously when he saw Laurel, while Horst jumped up eagerly and said, "Sit next to me, Lorelei."

As soon as the last word was out of his mouth, he cast a quick, guilty glance at his uncle, knowing he'd done something forbidden. But Conrad seemed not to have heard him. "I'm glad to see that you are better, Fräulein," he said formally. "But don't let Horst tire you, or you'll soon have a relapse."

"I don't tire you, do I?" Horst appealed to Laurel. "I'm *good* for you, aren't I?"

"So good that she ended up with a broken ankle," Conrad observed wryly.

"That wasn't Horst's fault," Laurel retorted, giving Conrad a significant glance. He colored and said no more.

"Of course it wasn't Horst's fault," Johanna said, flashing Laurel a look full of gratitude. "I don't know why you must be so hard on the child, Conrad."

"Hard on him?" Conrad echoed, looking ruffled. "Is it being hard to point out that he shouldn't run off alone and endanger himself and others—"

"Oh, let it drop," Laurel said. "Surely you've lectured the poor child enough already."

"How do you know I have?" Conrad demanded.

"Well, I'll bet you have," she hedged. It would have been rude to say that she couldn't imagine him overlooking the most minor incident of childish mischief.

Conrad glanced at Horst, who muttered, "Uncle Conrad didn't say anything about it."

Laurel stared at Conrad. He met her gaze with a look that showed he understood her surprise. A shadow passed briefly over his strong features, and he rose, pushing back his chair. "If you'll excuse me, I have work to do.'' He walked out, calling to the maid to bring some coffee to his study.

Laurel bit her lip, not quite understanding the atmosphere that had settled over the room, but realizing that Conrad had a thinner skin than she'd thought. She wished he'd given her a chance to apologize for having jumped to conclusions, but in the same moment she guessed that he'd departed in order to avoid the awkwardness of an apology.

After breakfast, Friederich wheeled her around the extensive grounds of the castle. He was a delightful companion, paying her outrageous compliments and making her laugh. But only half her mind was with him. The other half was with Conrad, wondering how soon she could give him the slip so she could see the baron—or simply thinking about Conrad himself with a persistence that disconcerted her. She decided that the eerie, ''otherworldly'' atmosphere of the Rhine must be getting to her, undermining her common sense.

Friederich drove her down into town and bought her lunch in a little café overlooking the river.

''You shouldn't spend so much time entertaining me,'' she protested. ''I'm sure you have a job to do.''

He made a face. ''I'm in the sales office of the family business. I admit it's not difficult, because our brandy practically sells itself, but there's more to it than 'teeth and charm,' no matter *what* Conrad says.''

''Conrad sounds like a tyrant.''

''It's better not to get on his wrong side,'' Friederich agreed. ''But he's not so bad. He's a good friend if you're in trouble.''

''I dare say you know all about being in trouble,'' she teased.

"I get into scrapes occasionally," he admitted. Then he caught her mischievous look and they both laughed. "In fact, quite a lot."

"Wine, women and song?"

"Women mostly. I tend to put them on pedestals which, according to Conrad, is the wrong thing to do. Conrad is severely practical about women. I can't imagine him ever admiring one that way."

"Never mind about him," Laurel said. "You're old enough to make up your own mind about your relationships."

"So I think. Unfortunately, however, Conrad keeps proving to be right. But not this time." He took her hand and looked intensely into her eyes. "Now I know I've found a woman who will stay on her pedestal and not turn out to have feet of clay."

Masking a desire to laugh, Laurel disengaged her hand. "I've got one foot made of plaster already," she said, pointing to her ankle.

With a wicked glint in his eye, Friederich took a pen from his pocket and leaned down to write something on the plaster cast. "There," he said triumphantly. "Now everyone will know how I feel about you."

"What nonsense!" she reproved him lightly. "You haven't known me long enough to feel anything."

"What does that matter? A moment can be enough to spark a love that lasts a lifetime."

"Or dies in five minutes."

"Don't interrupt me when I'm being poetic. Where was I?"

"Saying a moment can be enough."

"Ah, yes. A flash of lightning, a clap of thunder, and you're lost forever—"

"Or until your brother comes to rescue you."

"But perhaps it creeps up on you. You think you're safe, but you find yourself constantly thinking of one person, and you can't understand why—"

"That's enough," she said, with a sudden edge to her voice.

"Until you realize that the one who haunts your thoughts is the one you love—"

"I said that's enough," Laurel repeated firmly. "Let me have a look at what you've written."

She had to squint, because the words were upside down, but at last she made out two lines of verse:

"I cannot tell what it means,
This sadness that haunts me...."

"You shouldn't have done that," she said, exasperated.

"Do you recognize the words?"

"They're the opening lines of a poem called 'The Lorelei,' by Heine."

"Well done," Friederich said in surprise.

"That's not what your brother will say."

"Never mind about him," Friederich said, echoing her own words of a moment ago. "I'm old enough to make up my own mind about my relationships." He added, "If I want to listen to your siren song and die in your toils, why shouldn't I?"

"I think it's time we went home," she said emphatically.

He sighed as he rose reluctantly to his feet. "Never mind. Unrequited love is good for me. A man should suffer."

Laurel caught a glimpse of another side of Friederich later that evening when he sat down at the piano and began to play Brahms with subtle sensitivity. So, there was more to him than what appeared on the surface, she mused. When he'd finished growing up he'd be a prize for some lucky woman. She smiled as she contemplated his handsome head bent over the keyboard.

Gradually she became aware of another presence, and looked up to find Conrad watching her. He glanced at Friederich, then at her, and a look of wry cynicism crossed his features. To her annoyance, Laurel felt herself coloring at what he was obviously thinking.

A moment later, he strolled over and sat close to her wheelchair beside the window. "I trust you've had a pleasant day," he said courteously.

"Very pleasant, thank you. Your brother made sure of that, but I've told him he mustn't spend so much time with me in the future."

Conrad shrugged. "Oh, I imagine he'll do what he likes. He usually does. Luckily for him, he has charm—at least, so I'm told. So he gets away with it."

"I gather charm doesn't figure very highly on your list of accomplishments," Laurel said, irritated at his cool tone.

"I don't consider it an accomplishment at all. Charm is a gift. In the wrong hands it can be a weapon. Has he been exercising it on you, Fräulein?"

"I imagine he exercises it on everyone," she said casually. "I attach no importance to it."

"You're a wise woman." Conrad smiled, and suddenly Laurel experienced the same feeling she'd had before, when he'd carried her in his arms. For a moment the room swam and she had to close her eyes.

"What is it?" Conrad demanded at once, taking her hands.

"Nothing." She opened her eyes quickly and gave him a rather forced smile. She was intensely aware of the warm, strong clasp in which her hands were enfolded.

"You mustn't overtire yourself on your first day," he said. "I'm sending you to bed."

He wheeled her out of the room. In the hall, he stopped and called Helga on the internal telephone, then headed for Laurel's bedroom. Once there, he put an arm around her waist and helped her out of the chair and onto the bed. "Helga will be here in a moment to help you . . ."

Laurel looked up as Conrad's voice faded. His eyes were fixed on the lines from the "Lorelei" poem that Friederich had written on the plaster. For a moment his mouth tightened. Then he resumed speaking, but this time there was a chill in his voice. " . . . to help you prepare for the night. Ah, here she is. I hope you sleep well, Fräulein."

Without giving her a chance to reply, he strode out.

Chapter Three

After a week in the castle, Laurel was no closer to accomplishing her mission. In desperation she tackled Helga, but, as she'd feared, this proved futile. Helga looked furtively around the main hall, where Laurel had caught her, and said in a low voice, "I dare not let you into that room. I've been told not to."

"Couldn't you just look the other way?" Laurel pleaded.

"It's more than my job's worth to risk it," Helga said firmly. "And the same is true for Brigitta." Brigitta was the relief nurse. She was younger and more obliging than Helga, but just as fearful of Conrad's wrath.

They heard a car drawing up outside the castle, and in another moment Conrad appeared through the front door. For a moment the sunlight streamed after him, dazzling Laurel, so that she had to blink to make him out. He was casually dressed in a light, short-sleeved shirt that revealed his strong arms, with their short curling hairs, and the heavy gold watch on his left wrist.

He glanced briefly up at Helga, who had started to hurry up the stairs as soon as she saw him. "Well, did you get anywhere?" he asked Laurel politely.

"You know I didn't. Neither she nor Brigitta would dare disobey you."

"Naturally," he agreed, smiling faintly. "You were foolish to try."

"I tried because it's terribly important. There must be some way to make you understand, somehow. You can't possibly be as unyielding as you seem."

Conrad raised his eyebrows in cool irony. "Can't I? Why not?"

She sighed, baffled and exasperated, as she always felt when he confronted her with her own helplessness. "Because nobody could be," she said at last.

"I think you're discovering otherwise. A man ought to be unyielding when he's doing what he thinks is right."

Laurel craned her neck to look up at him, inwardly cursing the wheelchair, which put her at a distinct disadvantage when arguing with Conrad. "But maybe a man shouldn't be so rigid in his ideas of what's right," she suggested. "There's more than one 'right,' after all."

"Not in this case."

"You're so sure of yourself," she muttered crossly. "Hey, where are we going?" Conrad had taken hold of the wheelchair and begun pushing.

"To the terrace. I want to talk to you."

He wheeled her out onto the stone terrace that over-looked the gorge. Far below them, boats traveled up and down the Rhine, looking like tiny models. Laurel leaned over to watch them, momentarily distracted by the delightful sight.

He took advantage of her absorption to study her, and noticed that the pale, drawn look she'd had the first time she'd ventured out of bed had vanished. Her face was flushed with pleasure as she stared down into the gorge, then raised her head to the sky, closing her eyes and letting the warmth flood over her like a benediction. There was something so innocently pagan in the way she offered herself to the sun's caress that he couldn't help smiling despite his antagonism.

Suddenly, his smile faded and he drew in his breath at the way the light caught her long, silky hair, making it gleam like spun gold. Mingled with his admiration was a thread of something that was almost fear.

Nonsense, he told himself firmly. He'd never been afraid of anything. But he wished this woman hadn't come here, with her disturbing name and her even more disturbing appearance.

"Why do you persist?" he demanded suddenly. "How can you be so blind? Don't you understand that your attempts are useless?"

"Perhaps it's you who are blind," she responded. "Otherwise, you might realize that I wouldn't persist if it wasn't important."

"My grandfather is dying," Conrad growled. "Nothing can matter to him now."

"You couldn't be more wrong. It's *because* he's dying that it matters. *Please* listen to me. It's vital that I see him."

In her eagerness she'd reached out and caught hold of his arm. He looked down at her hand, then raised his eyes sharply to her face. The intensity he saw there caused a stab of unaccustomed emotion to shoot through him. What would it be like, he wondered, to care about something so much? To be so tuned in to life that you could cast caution aside and trust your feelings so completely?

But his sense of danger was too strongly developed to let him give an inch. He stiffened in resistance, and saw the way she blushed and removed her hand hastily. His bare arm was burning where she had touched him, and he had to overcome an impulse to seize her hand, lay it once more against his flesh, or draw it to his lips. "If you did see him," he demanded, "what would you say to him?"

"I told you, I have something to give to him, something I promised to deliver."

"And what do you expect a dying man to do?"

She hesitated before saying softly, "I expect him to be happy."

Anger darkened his face. "Don't try to talk to me in riddles," he snapped. "I'm a plain man and I don't like mysteries."

"Perhaps that's because you don't understand them."

He took a deep breath. "Fräulein, I'm trying to give you the benefit of the doubt, but you make that very difficult. Once and for all, will you tell me what it is you wish to deliver to my grandfather?"

"I don't know. It's wrapped. I've no idea what's inside."

He stared. "And you expect me to let you into his sickroom to torment him?"

"Is that really what you think of me?" she flashed. "That I'd *torment* a dying man?"

"Not, perhaps, deliberately but—very well, I withdraw the accusation and I apologize. But apart from that, I can only repeat what I said once before. If you will give this package to me, I will deliver it for you."

Laurel shook her head. "I think I'd better wait for a chance to deliver it myself."

"So you don't trust me to hand it over?"

"No," she responded simply.

He gave a wry grin. "How perceptive of you."

"How can I trust you when you don't trust me?"

"Why should I trust you when you're so secretive? At least tell me who gave you this package and made you promise to come here?"

She shook her head stubbornly.

"Why the devil not?" he demanded.

"Because you couldn't possibly understand. I think you're a man who doesn't understand much."

Conrad flinched and looked away from her. To his own surprise, her opinion hurt, and he felt as though she'd suddenly shut him out in the cold. He turned a pale face toward her. "Let's leave this subject before we have a more serious quarrel," he said. "I have a suggestion that may help you out of your present difficulties. I want Horst to learn good English and since he's very fond of you, you'd make the ideal teacher. His last tutor was useless at the subject."

"Why must he have a tutor at all? Why not send him to school?"

He drew in a sharp breath and spoke through clenched teeth. "I will not justify myself to you. I am doing what I think best for my nephew."

"And suffocating the poor child in the process. He has all my sympathy."

"No doubt that's why you told him I was a 'terrible fusspot'" Conrad snapped.

"Did I? I don't recall."

"You said it on the first day, when you were scheming to get into the castle."

"Oh yes," she said, remembering. For her, only one aspect of that day was clear: the memory of being carried in his arms, her body crushed against his hard chest, absorbing the heat of his flesh and the sense of vibrant masculinity and danger. Everything else had blurred. But that one remark of hers, tossed out casually, had evidently rankled with Conrad.

"Perhaps you only slandered me to win him over to your side," Conrad observed. "But whatever the reason, when you're teaching him, please be good enough to keep your opinion of me to yourself."

"I haven't yet agreed to teach him," she protested, nettled by his presumption that she, like everyone else, would fall in with his plans.

"But you will when you hear what I'm prepared to pay."

"I don't want money."

"Nonsense. I'm not asking for your charity," he said sharply.

"It wouldn't be charity," she pointed out. "You're feeding and housing me. It's only right that I should do something in return."

"You'll be paid a proper fee," Conrad said firmly, "and that's the end of it. You forget that I went through your things when you were taken off the boat. I discovered that you live in a part of London that— how can I put this without offending you?"

"Why bother to try?" she asked sarcastically.

"Very well, you are—in your English phrase—'as poor as a church mouse'. Otherwise you wouldn't be living in that down-at-heel area."

"Actually, I'm far from poor," Laurel said, thinking of Anna's picture and the hundred thousand pounds she could have when she sold it. "In fact I'm very well-off."

"Of course you are," Conrad agreed in a soothing tone. "You're a wealthy eccentric who likes living in a shabby area."

"I recently came into an inheritance—"

"I'm very happy for you, but it won't change my decision to pay you a proper salary for the job. Please don't argue with me. My mind is made up."

"All right," Laurel muttered, exasperated. "Have it your own way."

"How ungracious you are, Fräulein!" Conrad said with a mocking grin. "Since you're so much better, I ought to send you home now. Instead, I've given you the chance to stay here, where you may yet outwit me and scale the tower. You should be obliged to me."

"Not at all. You wouldn't have done it if you'd really thought I was going to succeed."

Conrad acknowledged this with a wry grin, but the wryness was directed at his own confusion. He was a logical man, and now his own behavior disturbed him. Why hadn't he heeded the warnings of his instincts, and rid himself of her as soon as possible? But, he argued with himself, it was wiser to keep her here until he'd discovered what she was up to. In this manner, he explained away his own inner contradictions.

"I thought you might have been worried about being away from your job in England," he said with a shrug.

"I work free-lance. I'm independent."

"A person then? Surely there is someone to worry himself about you?" As he spoke, Conrad looked not at her but across the gorge.

"No one," she said simply. "I live alone." She'd thought she was accustomed to Anna's loss, but as she said it, she realized suddenly that she really was alone. The little apartment where they'd lived contentedly together would never again ring to the sound of her grandmother's affectionate scolding, or her unexpectedly robust laughter. And suddenly a wave of sadness washed over her, and her voice shook before she could control it.

Conrad turned his head sharply just in time to see her brush the corner of her eye. "I see," he said gently.

"No you don't," Laurel said, blowing her nose. "I know what you're thinking, and you're quite wrong."

"According to you, I'm wrong about everything," he said. "Are you telling me that a man isn't involved? I can't believe it. When a woman has the looks you do, there are always men involved—men who can't help themselves."

"You sound as though other men are a different species from you," she protested. "Doesn't it ever get uncomfortable perching on that lofty peak?"

He flinched at the irony in her tone, and it took him a moment to compose himself enough to say coolly, "Let's say I managed to avoid the foolishness that Friederich is now going through. It's only good sense to stay clear of danger."

"Then I pity you," she said, meaning it, "because you know nothing."

An unfamiliar bitter impulse made him say, "I see. Then no doubt you're anxious to get back to him."

"There's no 'him'. The person who left me was my grandmother. I loved her very much, and she died," Laurel said simply. "I believe even you can recognize that kind of love."

"Yes," Conrad said after a moment in which there was complete silence. "I apologize. I had no right to—" He took a sharp breath. "Death is always hard, but some deaths are unbearable." Laurel looked up at him, wondering at the note of deep pain in his voice, but he hurried on, "Perhaps I'd better leave before I offend you any further." He walked away, but before he left, Laurel felt a light touch on her shoulder, as a gentle hand briefly rested there.

Later that day, Horst came scampering for his first lesson, overjoyed that his new friend was going to stay. He also delivered an envelope from Conrad, which contained an advance on wages and a businesslike statement concerning the rate at which she would be paid. Laurel's eyes opened wide at the amount, which was more than generous.

Never having taught before, she had to play it by ear. She started by testing her pupil's abilities. It turned out that Horst knew some basic English, so Laurel encouraged him to chatter about whatever interested him, and supplied the English words where necessary. In this way, she discovered that the chief thing on his mind was the upcoming carnival, a combination of events, rides and a beer festival that was held in Hargen every year. "There's a procession with everyone wearing funny costumes. You have to be nine before you can join in. I was nine last year, but Uncle Conrad still says I'm too young," Horst complained.

"Oh yes, you mentioned it the first day we met," Laurel reminded him.

"I've got a wonderful monster costume that mother bought me."

"Well, if your mother agrees to your taking part, I don't see what business it is of your uncle's," Laurel said, frowning.

"She said I could at first, but then Uncle Conrad talked her out of it. People always do what he wants." Horst sighed. "Can't you persuade him, Lorelei?"

"I'm not much good at persuading him, I'm afraid," Laurel said wryly. "Why don't you ask your Uncle Friederich to try?"

"Who's talking about me?" Friederich demanded, appearing in the doorway. Horst greeted him happily, evidently feeling that he would be an ally. But when the problem was explained, Friederich shook his head. "Conrad would get annoyed if I even brought it up," he said. He tweaked Horst's hair. "Don't sulk, youngster. You'll see plenty of the carnival."

"Yes, but it won't be the same," Horst said sadly.

Friederich settled down with the air of someone who'd come to stay. "Has Conrad given you the afternoon off?" Laurel asked, amused.

"He didn't exactly give it," Friederich said carefully. "I just sort of—"

"Took it?"

"Exactly." He beamed.

"How is Horst ever to learn responsible behavior if you don't set him a good example?" she chided playfully.

"You're beginning to sound like Conrad," he protested. "And you misunderstand my good intentions.

My English needs brushing up, so I came to join the lesson."

"Nonsense, I've heard you. You speak English fluently."

"No, honestly, teacher, I need intensive coaching."

Seeing that it was useless, Laurel gave up. The three of them had a merry afternoon until Johanna came to tell Horst to get ready for dinner.

"Not yet," Horst pleaded, moving closer to Laurel. "I want to stay with Lorelei."

"You'll see her at supper," his mother reminded him, smiling at Laurel. "Come along now."

"It's delightful the way that boy adores you," Friederich observed when they were alone.

"I was afraid Johanna might resent me for being so close to him, but she doesn't seem to, I'm glad to say."

"Johanna has her own way of looking at things. She's got an acid tongue, and it doesn't do to get on her wrong side, but she worships Horst to the point of idolatry and thinks only the best is good enough for him. Since you're obviously making him happy, she isn't jealous."

"But does she think it makes him happy to be shut up here with no friends of his own age to play with? Why doesn't she stop Conrad from being so strict with him?"

"You can't blame Conrad for being over-protective. He protects everyone, it's his nature. And a few years ago, Horst was abducted and we had a ransom demand. Luckily, the boy was so young that he didn't understand what was happening. He wasn't snatched, but enticed away with toys, and the police got him back before he had time to get scared. But Conrad has taken no chances since then."

"Oh, heavens!" Laurel said. "So that's the reason! And I've been hurling criticisms at him. Why on earth didn't he just explain?"

"Explain?" Friederich mocked. "Conrad *explain*? How little you know him. Superior beings like my brother don't justify themselves to lesser mortals. They don't care whether we approve of them or not, as long as we do what they tell us."

"Yes, I gathered that. 'Lesser mortals' means everyone else in the world, doesn't it?"

"More or less. The only person Conrad looks up to is our grandfather."

"How is the baron now?"

"Pretty much the same. I was allowed in for a few minutes this morning. He just lies there, apparently quite peaceful. Whenever he hears the door, he opens his eyes almost eagerly, as if he was expecting someone. But then he closes them again at once."

Laurel was silent, thinking of the old man patiently waiting for the right person to come to him, always hopeful and, so far, always disappointed. "A penny for your thoughts," Friederich teased.

"I was wondering how to get to see your grandfather. It's what I'm really here for."

"I know," Friederich said.

"I suppose Conrad told you not to help me." Laurel sighed. "Friederich, please, couldn't you just forget to lock the door next time you come down?"

"Darling, I'd do anything to help me—even risk Conrad's wrath—but it would be useless. That tower has a winding staircase. Even with my help, you'd never get a wheelchair up there. Didn't Conrad tell you that?"

"No, he didn't," she said crossly. "He's been watching me waste my efforts, knowing I'd never get past the first step. Well, that settles it. The sooner I get my crutches, the better."

"And *then* what do you think is going to happen?" Friederich asked, looking alarmed.

Laurel gave him her most winning smile. "Then I think you're going to help me up the tower stairs," she said.

Friederich hesitated and a look of mischievous cunning came into his eyes. "Is that my lady's command?" he asked, leaning closer.

"Of course."

"*Are* you my lady?"

"That isn't the issue right now. Let's discuss that later," Laurel stalled. With so much at stake, she felt heaven would forgive her a little ambiguity. Besides, Friederich's lighthearted manner convinced her that he was only playing at romance.

"I'll look forward to that discussion," he said. "In the meantime, how about your giving me a small token on account?" Quick as a flash, he tipped up her chin and laid his lips lightly on hers. He didn't try to take the kiss any further, and Laurel allowed it for a moment before gently disengaging herself.

Then she looked up and nearly cried out in dismay as she saw Conrad standing in the doorway looking at them with a sardonic expression on his face. "I came to find out what happened to you two," he said, "but perhaps you'd prefer to be left alone."

"We would, much rather," Friederich said promptly, trying to keep hold of Laurel's hand. She snatched it back, dismayed to realize she was blushing.

"I suppose this is where you were all afternoon, when you should have been working?" Conrad demanded of his brother, then turned to Laurel. "Perhaps I didn't make myself clear, Fräulein? It's Horst you've been hired to teach."

"Don't blame Laurel just because I played truant," Friederich said gallantly.

"You do it too often. It sets a poor example to your nephew."

This was so nearly an echo of Laurel's own words to Friederich earlier that she gasped. Friederich flashed her a devilish glance, and though she tried hard to avoid it, her lips twitched. Conrad watched her through narrowed eyes.

"We're just coming in to dinner," Laurel told him hastily.

"I'll leave then," Conrad said, giving her a telling look before departing.

"I think we should be a little more careful," she told Friederich.

"Never fear, fair lady. Our passion will remain a secret," he promised theatrically.

"Don't be ridiculous, Friederich," she declared firmly. Then, when he seemed about to object, she said, "Let's go in now. We don't want him coming back."

She was furious with herself, with Friederich and with the mischievous fate that had brought Conrad in at that precise instant. Earlier that day there had been a moment when he'd almost softened toward her. Now she was back to square one, associated in his mind with Friederich's "foolishness," and with danger. Now he would be twice as wary of her.

Chapter Four

Dinner was an uncomfortable meal during which Friederich persisted in giving Laurel knowing smiles, while she tried not to see them. Conrad seemed oblivious, and as soon as the meal was over, he declared he had work to do and left.

Laurel wheeled herself determinedly after him and knocked on his study door. In answer to his call, she opened the door and tried to maneuver herself through, but the side of the chair hit the doorjamb, and she had to reverse awkwardly. Conrad was evidently surprised to see her, but he came to her rescue and wheeled her in. The office was a large room with gothic windows, an open fireplace and a medieval atmosphere.

"What can I do for you, Fräulein?" he enquired.

"I wish you'd stop calling me Fräulein. It's so formal."

"Sometimes a little formality can be a good thing. It helps one to remember where the battle lines are drawn."

"But I don't want to fight you."

"I don't want it, either. Unfortunately, Fate seems to have cast us as opponents."

"I think it's too easy for people to blame Fate for their own stubbornness," she retorted spiritedly.

He regarded her uncertainly. "If this is another one of your tricks..."

"I've come here to apologize."

"It *is* another one of your tricks. What are you apologizing for? Making love to my brother?"

She was about to declare that she had no interest in Friederich but caught herself, realizing that this would invite awkward questions. Conrad watched her face with a cynical smile that suggested he was reading her thoughts. "Perhaps it's Friederich you should apologize to?" he suggested innocently.

"I don't know what you mean."

"I think you do, but let's not go into that. I'll only say that if you bring my little brother to the point of defying me, I'll really believe he's in love."

"I didn't come here to talk about him. I came to apologize for misjudging you. Friederich told me that Horst was kidnapped a few years ago." She saw his face tighten with displeasure, but added reproachfully, "Why didn't you tell me about it yourself?"

"Because I don't feel obliged to explain myself to every stranger who comes knocking at the door—Have I said something funny?" His sharp eyes had picked up Laurel's fleeting smile.

"My mind was wandering," she said quickly. Actually, she'd been laughing at Friederich's uncannily accurate analysis of his brother's attitude, but it would be wise not to tell Conrad that. "Anyway, I'm not a stranger now. Ask Horst."

"Have you spoken to him about this?" he asked sharply.

"Not a word."

"Thank you for that, at least. The less said about what happened to him the better. I don't want his mind darkened with fears." He looked down at her as if trying to decide something, then said abruptly, "You may not believe this, but he is very dear to me."

"Of course I believe you. Why shouldn't I?"

He gave her a wry smile. "Because in your mind I'm every kind of monster."

"Not *every* kind, just the kind that likes to make all decisions—including other people's."

"I'm afraid I'm rather in the habit of making decisions. I've been acting head of this family for some years, ever since my grandfather began turning responsibilities over to me."

"I think the whole idea of a family 'head' is rather feudal."

"Indeed," he said in a chilly, courteous voice that was like the closing of a door.

"Oh, stop being so darned polite," Laurel said, exasperated. "It would be more honest if you came right out and ordered me to mind my own business."

"I thought that was what I was doing," he said. "In fact, it's what I'm sure I've been doing since the first day we met—with very little success."

"I suppose I'm a bit like you, really," she said, considering. "I can't resist telling other people how they ought to live their lives."

He glared at her. "What a dreadful woman you are," he said, then sighed in resignation. "But let's not quarrel any more. Give me your opinion about this."

He'd taken an unlabeled bottle from his desk, and was pouring a small measure of topaz-colored liquid into a heavy crystal goblet. He handed it to Laurel, who took a sip and found it a smooth and delicious brandy. "It's one of this year's blends," Conrad explained. "Not the best, but a good start."

"I think it's superb," Laurel declared.

"For any other make, it would be superb. For Feldstein brandy, it's moderate," Conrad observed, with sublime unawareness of his own arrogance. He held up his glass. "Let's drink to our truce." They clinked glasses and drank.

"Horst has been telling me about the English lesson you gave him this afternoon," Conrad said. "I take it, then, that you agree to my suggestion?"

"I'll gladly teach him. However, I *don't* agree to the money part."

"I wish you could have seen how happy Horst was as he described your lesson," Conrad said, apparently not registering her objection. "He enjoyed it tremendously, and that means a lot to me. I know how confined he feels. I don't dare take risks with his safety, but you can help him. You can open windows and show him new worlds. Be his friend. He needs that very much."

"Of course I will. I think he's a delightful child."

"He is, isn't he?" Conrad said with sudden eagerness. "He's so like his father. Markus would have smuggled himself onto that boat, just as Horst did. When we were children, he was always the one in trouble, and I was always the one who rescued him." He hesitated a moment, as if weighing a risk, then abruptly leaned over his desk, picked up a large photograph in a brass frame, and handed it to her.

Laurel studied the face of the young man in the picture. Like his brothers he was handsome, and his grin held some of Friederich's mischief. But there was another quality, a hint of seriousness that underpinned the laughter and made him more like Conrad.

She looked up to find him watching her expression. His eyes were suddenly full of a wintry loneliness that touched her heart. Now she understood what he'd meant when he'd said that some deaths were unbearable. Forgetting everything except his obvious unhappiness, she said softly, "You loved your brother very much, didn't you."

"I was closer to him than I've ever been to another human being," Conrad said simply. "When he died . . ." He gave a little shrug that was more eloquent than words.

Laurel was silent. She longed to comfort him. But although he had allowed her to see a little way into his private pain, she knew that this reserved man wouldn't let all his barriers fall so easily. If she ventured too far, she would be rebuffed. "How did he come to die so young?" she asked at last.

"He fell while rock climbing, but if it hadn't been that, it would have been something else. He loved risking his neck. Just like Horst. Like his father, he'll run after every mad idea that takes his fancy. That's why I must keep him safe."

"But you can't bring your brother back by protecting his son," Laurel said, knowing she was treading on dangerous ground.

For a moment she thought he might chastise her, but he only sighed. "Is that what I'm doing? I don't know. I can't forgive myself for not having looked after Markus better than I did."

"But he was a grown man. Why should it be your responsibility to look after him?"

"Perhaps because, as you suggested, I like to make everyone's decisions for them. It's the way I am." Conrad's voice dropped then, as he said, "Even now I relive his death and work out ways I could have made it all happen differently."

"But you couldn't have," Laurel said gently. "No one can control another person's life as much as that. You only hurt yourself by thinking that you could have had that much power."

"Maybe you're wiser than I," Conrad agreed. "Who can say? But I was with Markus as he lay dying. He took my hand and begged me to protect his wife and son. He could hardly speak, but he fought to get the words out, and I promised him. I almost failed in that promise once, when Horst was kidnapped. Thank God I was given a second chance, and I won't fail again." He looked thoughtful for a moment. "He's been talking to you about this carnival procession, hasn't he?"

"Yes, he's miserable about being left out. Look, call me an interfering busybody if you like, but I think you should pull out all stops to make it possible."

"And if he gets snatched in the crowd?"

"Make sure he doesn't. Take part with him. Then you can keep an eye on him all the time."

She almost laughed at his outraged look. "Are you suggesting that *I* dress up in a carnival costume?" he asked when he found his voice. "Have you any idea how they dress?"

"If you don't want to do it, ask Friederich to help. He wouldn't mind dressing up. Get Boris, the gatekeeper, as well. He's built like a gorilla. It's not enough to keep Horst safe, you've got to keep him happy as well."

"Meaning that I don't care for his happiness?" he asked, his eyes burning.

"I know you care, but you're not very—well, imaginative." She was careful to pick words that would not antagonize him.

To her relief, he smiled ruefully. "I suppose I must plead guilty to that. I thought loving him was enough, but perhaps—" he broke off with a sigh.

"You love Horst because he's Markus's son, don't you?" Laurel asked.

"I suppose I do, but I also love him for his own sake. He may have inherited his mischief from his father, but he has plenty on his own account."

"Yes, I've discovered that," Laurel said, marveling at the change that had come over Conrad in the last few minutes. There was a gentleness, even a tenderness, about him that contrasted with his normal manner. She wondered if she was more susceptible to brandy than she'd thought, because a delicious warmth was stealing through her. Then Conrad smiled, not with his mouth but with his eyes, and she knew the brandy had nothing to do with it. He was looking at her in a puzzled way, as though a strange and startling thought had just occurred to him. For a moment, she was sure he was going to speak.

"Can I come in?" Friederich asked from the doorway, and the atmosphere shattered. Laurel's blissful feeling drained away as he reminded her, "You promised me a game of chess this evening."

"Since when did chess interest you?" Conrad demanded sharply.

Friederich gave Laurel a significant glance. "Since I discovered that my lady is an expert."

"Then you'd better hurry along," Conrad said with a shrug. "Thank you for coming, Fräulein. It's been very interesting talking to you."

Laurel allowed herself to be wheeled away, but inside her there was an empty feeling where happiness recently had been. She tried to shake herself free of the strange melancholy, but without success. It was irrational to feel this way. Nothing had happened, and yet everything had happened. Conrad had smiled at her, and for a moment she had had a glimpse behind his prickly, defensive barrier.

What she had discovered there had intrigued her, made her long to explore further until she reached his lonely, well-guarded heart. Perhaps even that would open to her, and she could enter and discover her own heart's joy. For, despite the antagonism that ran like a thread of fire through their relationship, something was telling her that from now on there would be no fulfillment without Conrad.

Friederich's voice shattered her thoughts. "That's the third time I've asked you if you want some coffee."

Laurel came out of her reverie to discover that she was in the drawing room. "I'm sorry," she said quickly. "No coffee, thank you. And would you mind if we didn't play chess?"

"Anything to please you," he said gallantly. "What would you like to do?"

"Suppose you play the piano?"

"Of course." Friederich sat down and began to run his fingers over the keys.

Laurel gradually felt herself begin to relax a little. At least this way she didn't have to talk to him. Until now she'd enjoyed Friederich's merry nonsense, but suddenly it made her feel tense. She looked at him, absorbed in the music, and wondered why her heart couldn't respond to this handsome, delightful boy instead of...

"I'm so glad to find the chance to talk to you," Johanna whispered, slipping into a chair beside her. "I wanted to say how pleased I am to see Friederich courting you. He's very young, of course, and like most young men a little restless, but the right wife will make him settle down."

"But it's not like that," Laurel protested.

Johanna made a deprecating gesture. "Of course, I realize that he hasn't said anything definite to you yet, and until he does—well, let's leave it there. I just thought it might relieve your mind to know that his family approves."

She was evidently quite serious, and Laurel had to check the words of amazement that rose to her lips. She'd known that many aristocratic Germans still took a fairly rigid view of who was suitable to marry into their families, but it was a shock to actually encounter this attitude. As she was unable to speak her mind, she settled for defensive irony. "I wonder if Conrad would approve."

Johanna nodded. "I thought that might be worrying you, and of course it's very proper that you should consider his views. The von Feldsteins have always taken an extremely correct attitude to family alliances..."

"That rules me out," Laurel said tartly. "I haven't got a title."

"I was about to say that they also move with the times," Johanna added. "You're such a ladylike person that no one could possibly object to you."

Laurel stared in disbelief, but Johanna seemed oblivious to the possibility that anyone might find her words offensive. "Have you discussed this with Conrad?" Laurel asked at last.

"Not exactly, but I know he feels Friederich needs a steadying influence. And I hope it happens soon," Johanna said with a wistful sigh that made her seem human again. "It would be so nice for me to have a woman to talk to."

"Perhaps Conrad will marry," Laurel pointed out.

"Oh no," Johanna said quickly. "Conrad will never marry. He thinks love is a kind of sickness, and he's very good at avoiding entanglements."

"What about his family duty?" Laurel asked dryly.

"You mean an heir? But there is already an heir." Johanna's eyes rested fondly on a portrait of Horst that hung above the piano. "No, Conrad distrusts women too much ever to marry. I've heard him say so, many times."

The next day when Conrad came into the turret that housed his grandfather's quarters he noticed the door to the anteroom standing open. "What are you doing here?" he demanded, finding Horst inside.

"Mother took me up to see Grandpa, but she only let me stay a moment. She says Grandpa's dying, but he just seems very sleepy."

"He *is* dying," Conrad said, laying a gentle hand on the boy's shoulder. "When the time comes, I hope he'll just fall asleep peacefully and know nothing."

"When will the time come?" Horst asked, with the honest curiosity of a child.

"When he's ready, and only he knows when that will be. In the meantime, we must do all we can to keep trouble away from him." Conrad eyed his nephew sharply. "Did you tell him anything about Fräulein Blake?"

"No, he just looked at me for a moment, and closed his eyes again. Then, Mother sent me away."

"And you came here." Conrad looked up at the picture of the Lorelei. "I suppose I can guess why."

"It *is* her, Uncle. Truly it is."

"There's a faint resemblance," Conrad conceded reluctantly. "But the rest is your imagination." He knelt so that his face was on a level with Horst's and spoke earnestly. "Horst, never mention this likeness again, especially to your grandfather. To be the Lorelei is no recommendation in this family." Horst nodded obediently. Conrad studied his face for a moment. At last he said, "Does it really matter so much to be in the procession?"

Horst nodded.

Conrad sighed ruefully. "I suppose it's in the family blood. Your father and I used to take part in that procession when we were younger. We used to go as the two giants, Fasolt and Fafner."

"*You*, Uncle?" Horst's incredulity was so frank and spontaneous that, for a moment, Conrad caught a glimpse of himself through the child's eyes, and the vision made him wince.

"Yes," he said. "It doesn't sound very likely now, does it? But that's what we did, and we had a wonderful time. Your father was only a year younger than I, and we were great friends. There hasn't been a day since his death that I haven't missed him." He put his hands on Horst's shoulders. "I've never spoken to you about your father before, have I?"

Horst shook his head, looking at Conrad in wonder.

"I should have. One day soon we must talk, and I'll tell you what he was like as a child—how much like *you* are now. Well, I suppose I must find a way for you to be in the procession. I don't know what I'm going to do, but—" He broke off, gasping for breath as Horst flung his arms ecstatically around his neck. "All right, all right," he said hurriedly. "Now run along."

Horst pranced away, shouting joyfully, and Conrad became lost in thought. He could still feel the strong young arms clutched tightly around his neck, and the smooth cheek pressed against his own. How long was it since Horst had shown him such spontaneous affection? Something in Conrad's strong, unyielding nature had been moved almost to tears by the emotional gesture.

He wondered how this had come about. His sternest resolve had been overturned by forces he didn't understand, and somehow he couldn't help being glad. As if by association, he raised his head and looked intently at the Lorelei, a troubled frown in his eyes. There was mystery in the lovely features, and also a deceptive sweetness that was more alarming than overt cruelty. A man could gaze and gaze at that enigmatic face, lost, and content to be so, until he was enticed to his doom. Did the sailor in the little boat below realize how close he was to the rocks, Conrad wondered? Did he care, as long as he was held in that enchantment? And did he count his life well lost in return for a brief moment of bliss?

As if in a dream, Conrad reached out to touch the streaming golden hair. But his fingertips encountered only paint and canvas, and he snatched his hand back with a start. Abruptly, he left the room.

Later that day, the anteroom door was locked, and the key vanished.

Chapter Five

Two days later, Laurel abandoned the wheelchair for crutches, and spent the afternoon practicing walking in the big hall. As she paced, a growl overhead made her look up to see a small figure in medieval clothes. He scampered down until he was level with her, and thrust a hideous gargoyle face over the banister. "Grrr!"

Laurel laughed. "It's magnificent, Horst. You'll scare everyone into fits."

Horst pulled off the gargoyle mask. "Will I really?"

"There'll be nothing in the procession to match you," she promised. "I'm so glad your uncle said yes."

Horst nodded and beamed at her. "Thank you, Lorelei."

"Don't thank me. I didn't even know he'd changed his mind until you told me."

"But you did it. I know you did," he leaned toward her and said in a conspiratorial whisper. "Because you're the Lorelei, even though I'm not supposed to say so.''

Friederich came in at that moment and saved her from having to respond. He cringed in mock-terror when Horst growled at him, and they all laughed. Then he said to Laurel, "I left work early to see if you were steady enough for a pleasure trip. I'd like to take you to see the distillery."

She agreed at once, less out of interest in the distillery than because she wanted to talk to Friederich alone.

But as they drove down the steep, sloping road to the river, he forestalled her by saying apologetically, "I'm afraid my lady is going to be disappointed in me."

"Tell me," Laurel said, resignedly. "Or shall I guess?"

"Conrad has threatened me with dire consequences if I help you get to our grandfather."

"Couldn't you just disobey him?" she pleaded.

"No, I couldn't," Friederich said with a shudder. "I'm not as brave as you."

Laurel sighed, although she'd been half-expecting this. Once again, Conrad had been one step ahead of her. Everything would have been easy if she dared to tell him the truth. But all her instincts warned that it would only make him more determined than ever to keep her out, even to the point of ejecting her from the house. She couldn't risk it.

After driving along the bank for five miles, they reached the cluster of long, white buildings where the brandy was made. Nearby was a small, private railway station where the precious liquid started its journey to different parts of the world. Friederich led her under a stone archway and into the main building, where she found herself in a large room dominated by four huge copper vats in the center. Smaller vats lined the walls, and above their heads was a gallery with more vats.

"We begin with wine that our agents buy all over Europe," Friederich explained. "It's all mixed together in those vats, which are heated to the temperature at which alcohol evaporates, so it separates from the water. We get rid of the water and cool the alcohol until it returns to liquid, but now it's far more potent.

"We then repeat the whole process to produce an even more refined brandy. The best of that is put into barrels of a very special oak. It stays there for several years. I'll get the keys from the customs men and show you the cellar."

He departed before Laurel could speak. When he returned with the keys, she asked, "Did you say 'customs men'?"

"That's right. Spirits carry a heavy tax, so customs has an office in the building. They keep eagle eyes on the book work and guard the cellar keys. No one gets them without explaining why they need them. There's even closed-circuit television so that we can't sneak down for a duty-free glass without them knowing."

They descended into the cellar by a small elevator, then made their way along a white-painted brick passage until they reached an iron gate. Looking up, Laurel saw a camera fixed into the ceiling. As she limped into the cellar where the barrels were stacked high, the heady scent of brandy washed over her, so powerful that it stopped her in her tracks. "The wood is porous," Friederich explained. "So some always evaporates into the air. These barrels haven't been here very long, so the smell is quite light—"

"It is?" Laurel gasped.

"Comparatively speaking," he chuckled. "But over here—" he unlocked another gate and led her into a second chamber, where there were more barrels "—these have been maturing for four years, and you can tell."

The odor was a pungent mixture of sweetness, spices, and herbs. Friederich grinned at the sight of Laurel inhaling carefully. "You could almost get tipsy from standing here and just breathing," he said.

"I think I already am."

He put an arm around her waist. "Is it making you giddy?"

"I can manage, thank you," she said firmly.

"Let me give you a hand."

"Friederich, I don't need a hand."

He dropped his head to whisper in her ear, "Well, there's no harm if I give you one anyway, is there?"

Conrad had known today was going to be bad. He was due for a session of paperwork with Stefan, the customs officer, and he knew the papers would contain bad news. To make it worse, Stefan was also a good friend, and therefore would present the hard truth with a friend's frankness. After a day of studying accounts, Conrad faced the fact that things were even worse than he'd feared.

"It's not really my job to comment," Stefan said with a sigh. "I'm only here to make sure the duty is paid. But I can't look at these figures without seeing that your grandfather let things deteriorate."

"He refused to compromise on quality," Conrad growled, "and for that I respect him." He looked up sharply as the door opened. "Yes, what is it?"

"Can I have the keys to the cellar?" Friederich asked.

"Reason for visit?" Stefan enquired, pulling a form toward him.

Friederich grinned. "Entertaining a beautiful lady."

"I'll put 'public relations,'" Stefan said, "as I always do."

"I know what you're thinking," Friederich said defensively. "But this one really is different."

"Then you'd better not keep her waiting," Conrad observed, without looking up.

When Friederich had gone, Stefan resumed, "I respect the old man too, but he thought if he concentrated on quality, the profits would take care of themselves. Unfortunately, that's not true, and the place should have been run far more economically than it was. He insisted on the barrels being made of the most expensive oak...."

"Because essences in the wood act on the liquid, so the wood has to be the best," Conrad interrupted patiently. "That's why we use small barrels, so that as much of the liquid as possible is in direct contact with the wood, and no barrel is used more than four times. But we recoup some of the cost by selling the used barrels to other distilleries that make cheap brandy."

"I understand all that, but—Conrad, are you listening?"

"Yes," Conrad said hastily, tearing his gaze away from the bank of television screens that showed the cellars. Through the corner of his eye, he'd watched Friederich and Laurel get out of the elevator and approach the gate. When she'd suddenly looked up directly into the camera, he'd flinched, almost as though she could sense he was watching her. With her long,

fair hair turned to silver by the black-and-white camera, she looked uncannily like the Rhine maidens in the
picture books of his childhood.

"Since the baron put the running of the firm into
your hands, you can do a lot to set matters right,"
Stefan remarked.

"I won't use that power to betray his trust," Conrad said, his eyes on a screen that showed two figures
moving into the second chamber of the cellar. He
added mechanically, "There'll be no compromise over
the barrels."

"All right, but there are some other work practices
that could be modified...."

Conrad didn't hear him. He could see Laurel savor-
ing the exotic scent of the casks. Her eyes were closed
and her face illuminated by a mysterious half-smile.
Friederich moved closer to her.

"It's a pity about that evaporation," Stefan observed, following Conrad's glance. "It costs you a
million and a half bottles a year."

"The hell with that," Conrad muttered.

"But if you work out—" Stefan jumped back as
Conrad leaped to his feet, snatched up a spare set of
keys, and rushed from the room. Stefan studied the
screen where the two figures were struggling. Friederich had evidently tried to steal a kiss. The young woman's efforts to fend him off were hampered by her
crutches, but she fought gamely.

Conrad reached the cellars in double time. He could
hear the scuffle and Friederich's urgent imprecations,
"Please darling, you know I'm mad about you. I can't
bear it if you reject me—"

He heard Laurel, slightly muffled and breathless. "Friederich—no—" and then a gasp as if she had been silenced abruptly.

At that moment, Conrad rounded the last corner and came upon the two figures locked together, Friederich's mouth pressed passionately over Laurel's. In one step he reached them and hauled his brother away. Friederich's eyes, already hot with arousal, kindled into anger and he swung a punch. Conrad parried it easily, but Friederich's second effort was more successful and connected with his chin, sending him flying back until he cannoned into Laurel, knocking her off balance. She grabbed frantically at the barrels, but her stiff leg impeded her and she slid to the floor. She had no choice but to lie there watching helplessly as the men wrestled.

At last Conrad swung a vigorous left hook and in the next instant, Friederich was flat on his back. He jumped to his feet and tried to continue the fray, but Conrad thrust him against the wall. "Don't make me forget you're my brother," he said through clenched teeth.

For a moment they stared at each other, both tense and alert, their chests rising and falling. There the similarity ended. Friederich was already coming to his senses, but Conrad's gaze was wild, as if he were on the verge of doing something terrible.

Friederich gave an awkward laugh. "All right," he said. "I'm not crazy enough to go on."

Conrad dropped his hands. "It would be reprehensible enough to force yourself on a woman under ordinary circumstances," he snapped. "But when she's injured and can't defend herself . . ."

"Look, I'm sorry. I got carried away. I even forgot those damned cameras—"

"Then you're stupider than I thought. Now get out."

Friederich turned to Laurel and made a sound of dismay as he saw her struggling to get up from the floor. "I'm sorry, darling," he said earnestly, reaching out to her. "Let me—"

Conrad blocked his path. "Don't touch her," he said with deadly intensity.

Friederich took one look at his brother's livid face and stepped back. "All right, all right," he said. "If I'd known it was like that...I'm just going..." He departed quickly.

Conrad stood perfectly still a moment, as if trying to regain his composure. Then he dropped to one knee beside Laurel. "Put your hands on my shoulders," he said curtly.

She did so and felt him clasp her waist. He drew her up with him, not looking at her directly. When she was standing, he didn't release her at once but stood holding her. His jaw was set in a hard line, and Laurel could feel the heat raging through his body where it touched hers. "If you could fetch my crutches for me," she said slowly. "They got scattered—"

She fell silent as Conrad turned his gaze upon her. His eyes were brilliant, and he was breathing hard. When he spoke, his voice was harsh. "Are you all right?"

"Yes, thank you," she said, slightly breathless.

He was very close, looking down at her grimly. His usual stern composure had deserted him. His hair was tousled, his shirt torn open at the front, and a livid blue mark was beginning to appear over one cheekbone.

"I apologize," he said stiffly, "for the way—" He stopped, and bit his lip. Then he said violently, "It's about time someone put a stop to your tricks."

She stared. "I don't know what you mean. I never expected Friederich to get so intense."

Conrad laughed bitterly. "Stop pretending. You're not blameless. You know how he feels about you, and you've had your fun leading him on. But you turn cold when it suits you. I suppose you enjoy that even more. Does it give you a feeling of power?"

"Of course not," she said indignantly. "Flirting with a boy like him is just a harmless game."

"Did you ever wonder if it might mean more to him than that?" Conrad snapped. "Of course not. To you it was 'just a game', but the men of this family have suffered enough at the hands of women who treat love lightly. I won't let it happen again."

His closeness was affecting her, making it difficult to breathe. "I don't understand," she said.

"Then perhaps this will help you," he said, as his arms tightened around her. His mouth came down on hers, smothering her instinctive sound of surprise.

His lips were hard, kissing her without tenderness, but with fierce, desperate passion that made her head reel. Laurel felt his body vibrating with an emotion that felt like anger, and her own anger rose swiftly to meet it as she realized that this embrace was no more than an insult.

She managed to jerk her head free and mutter, "I'll tell you what I told your brother—let go of me at once."

"But I'm not my brother," he said through clenched teeth, holding her as tightly as ever. "He's a naive boy who fancies himself in love. That's a mistake I never make. I saw through love a long time ago, just as I saw through you."

"You know nothing about love *or* me," she flung at him.

He gave a short, cynical laugh. "I know that love is a fool's trick, and you're the kind of woman who doesn't like too much reality. You prefer to drop out before the game is spoiled, don't you? But I'm not your adoring little dog, like Friederich, and I'm not going to let you dodge *this* reality."

He covered her mouth again before she could speak, pressing her head back against the hard muscles of his arm that lay beneath her neck. She couldn't fight him, but suddenly she no longer wanted to. She knew now that she'd longed to feel his arms around her since the first moment. Whatever else had played along the surface of her mind, the thought of his firm mouth on hers had troubled her subconscious for a long time. Tremors went through her as she felt herself responding to the dark magic of his lips as they moved purposefully over her own.

Conrad fought to hang onto the last traces of his sanity, but all that mattered was the slim, vibrant body he held against his own. Laurel's mysterious loveliness had tortured him until today, when the sight of her with Friederich had made his control snap. Hot visions had danced before his eyes, making him ready to destroy any man—even his own brother—who dared touch her. After that, nothing could have stopped him from taking her into his arms.

And now she was there, honey and wine on his lips, soft warmth against his flesh, her resistance changing dangerously to sweet submission. He was caught in the shoals, lured by the siren's song, unable to break free, although he could see the rocks and feel himself being drawn nearer.

He was doing what he'd blamed Friederich for, using his strength to overpower a woman already weakened by injury. But he couldn't stop himself. Blind instinct drove him on to seek the heart of her and engulf himself in whatever secrets he found there. Nothing else mattered. He kissed her repeatedly, tracing the outline of her full mouth with its curves of promise and temptation. As his lips touched her, he murmured words that seemed to come from deep within himself. He didn't even know what he was saying. Spring and youth were in the scent of her skin, and the trembling of her body dazed his senses.

For so long, his existence had been ruled by caution. He'd kept his romances light, observed his obligations, rendered to each man exactly what he owed, and made sure that he owed nothing to any woman. Now it felt as though life itself had seized him and shaken him, thrusting him into a melee of confusing sensations and emotions, where he was no longer entirely himself, and where nothing was under his control.

He cupped her head in one hand, feeling her long tresses stream over his fingers like the endless flowing of the river, sweeping him onward to an unknown destination, leaving his everyday self far behind. An uncontrollable impulse made him bury his face in the silky hair, inhaling sweet fragrance, blissfully lost in her.

He kissed her face again, and he wasn't sure which of them willed it, but suddenly his tongue was in her mouth, sliding between softly parted lips. As her warm breath mingled with his, he felt madness engulf him.

Laurel melted with longing as his tongue found its way into her mouth, where it seemed to belong by right. Every part of her wanted to welcome him. She'd been made for this kiss, and now her whole being was concentrated in passionate response. Feelings for him had been growing within her, especially since the night when he'd relaxed his guard and let her share some of his private pain. Now they intermingled with a feverish desire that made her return caress for caress. As his tongue probed and explored her mouth, she pressed against him, feeling his heart beat against hers, willing them to beat to the same rhythm.

Feverishly, he moved one hand to the front fastening of her dress and opened the top button. She was searingly aware that he wanted to undress her, that he was on the verge of doing it, and her body ached with the desire to feel him touch her everywhere. It would be so hard to refuse him. And yet she must, for they were still far from the mutual trust upon which passion must rest. Without trust, their passion would end in bitterness.

She forced herself to fend him off, and at the same moment she felt him stiffen and take his mouth reluctantly from hers. He snatched his hand away and looked down at her face with shock, like a man who'd just escaped danger by a whisker. They drew apart, each seeing their own disturbance mirrored in the other's eyes.

"How do you like playing games now?" Conrad asked in an unsteady voice.

"Was that a game?" she said huskily.

He shook his head. He seemed dazed. "I'll get your crutches," he said at last.

Laurel clung to the barrels as he released her, and when he gave her the crutches, she knew he must be able to feel her trembling. His hands tightened over hers with a sudden convulsive movement, and there was a silence between them, echoing with the resonance of their mutual discovery. Then Laurel became aware of a slight whirring noise, and looked up at the camera in dismay.

Conrad exclaimed, realizing that his uninhibited behavior may have been observed. His eyes, meeting hers, were full of shock. For a moment, she thought she saw an accusation there, as though he blamed her for making him forget everything else but their passion. Then he took a deep breath and seemed to pull himself together. "Let's go," he said, standing back to let her pass, careful not to touch her.

He was quiet until they were upstairs. Then he said, "You'd better not go home with Friederich. Give him some time to think."

"Yes, I'd rather take a taxi."

"Of course you won't take a taxi," Conrad said firmly. "I'll drive you myself. There's a small garden through here where you can wait. I won't be long."

Laurel was glad of the chance to be alone to regain her equilibrium again.

She limped over to a wooden seat, barely hearing the voices that floated out of an open window overhead. It was peaceful to sit and contemplate the little pond with its goldfish that played occasionally on the surface. Her whole world was being turned upside down, and she no longer felt like herself.

What had happened between herself and Conrad had been inevitable, but it had still been shattering when it finally came. Even now she could feel the burning imprint of his mouth, and she wondered if he carried the memory of her on his own lips. She knew that he'd been shaken to the core by the discovery that she could destroy his control. Not only shaken—angered. He wanted to fight the turbulent emotions that had grown up between them. That much she was certain of. But whether he was strong enough to master his own feelings was as much a mystery to her as she guessed it was to him.

Before returning to the office, Conrad straightened his clothes and composed himself as best he could. Even so, he felt self-conscious as he entered, and from the way Stefan raised his eyebrows, he knew he had no secrets. "Let's get back to business," he growled.

"I thought that young woman was Friederich's little bit of fancy," Stefan observed ironically.

Conrad turned a threatening face on him. "*That's enough*. Whatever else she may be—" He hesitated. "Whatever else—she's no man's 'little bit of fancy.'"

"All right, all right," Stefan said, regarding him with interest.

Conrad reddened under his gaze. "Fräulein Blake is a guest in my house," he said stiffly. "I can't allow her to be referred to in that way."

"I see. You were just demonstrating your hospitality, and you were so intent on being a good host that you forgot the cameras."

"I repeat, let's stick to business," Conrad said in a hard voice.

"I *am* talking business. You can't afford to play around like that—not unless she's a wealthy woman."

"She hasn't a penny," Conrad snapped. "And I don't want to discuss her."

"Then let's discuss this. You're in debt up to the hilt with the bank. If you don't get a very large injection of cash by the tenth of next month, you'll have to mortgage the castle. I assume you have your grandfather's power of attorney?"

"Yes," Conrad said bleakly. "I can take whatever steps are necessary, but I hope—can we get back to the books?"

Stefan began to run his fingers down a column of figures, but Conrad's mind was elsewhere. He knew he should be concentrating on the threat to his home, but one vision obliterated all else: long, golden hair, running like the river through his fingers, clean and sweet-smelling as he pressed his face into it. Hair that gleamed, making a frame for a face with a mysterious, alluring smile . . . Laurel . . . Lorelei—

His head jerked up as he remembered the open window and the garden directly below, where he had left her. He rose quickly and looked out. The garden was empty.

"Let's call it a day," he told Stefan briefly.

"But I thought you wanted to go over—"

"Another time," Conrad said, taking his jacket and hurrying out.

Chapter Six

Conrad found Laurel in the lobby chatting to the receptionist. A few minutes later they were in his car, making their way toward Hargen. He drove through the little town and slowed as they neared the turn for the castle. Then, at the very last moment, he wrenched the wheel violently and the car swung back onto the road that ran along the riverbank. "We have to talk," he said in answer to her questioning look.

At last he turned into a small parking lot. "This is one of the best beer taverns on the Rhine," he explained.

It was a small, rustic place, with tables in the open air by the water. Conrad settled her and went to have a word with the proprietor.

Laurel hadn't spoken on the short journey. She was thinking about what she had overheard. She hadn't meant to eavesdrop, and she'd retreated from the garden as soon as possible, but she had an uncomfortable feeling of having pried into Conrad's secrets.

She saw him coming back, and in the rich wave of emotion that swept over her, everything was forgotten. She'd had romances before, but now she knew those experiences didn't count. None of the young men she'd kissed and laughed with had been able to engender this fierce eruption of feeling. Just the sight of Conrad walking toward her, the evening sun burnishing the russet of his hair, made her feel giddy with delight.

Conrad was already castigating himself for being a fool. He should have driven Laurel straight home, returned to the office, and worked late into the night seeking solutions to his problems. But now those problems seemed to dissolve, and only she was real. He was ashamed of the way he'd lost control and fought over her. He was ashamed that she'd witnessed it. He knew he was doing something dangerous, but he couldn't help himself.

They were served foaming beer in tall, colorful steins. Laurel tasted hers gingerly. She knew Conrad was watching her closely, his eyes narrowed as if appraising her, his face empty of the feeling that had so recently wracked him.

"You must forgive me for being confused," he said sardonically. "I'd gathered you and Friederich were on the verge of announcing your engagement."

Startled, she almost dropped her stein. "I—no, of course I'm not going to marry Friederich. Whatever gave you that idea?"

"Johanna asked for my approval."

"You don't mean to say she actually spoke to you about it?" Laurel asked, aghast.

"Do I gather that she spoke to you?"

"Only in passing. It was so absurd that I hardly listened. There's no question of my marrying Friederich. There never was."

"I wonder if Friederich knows that?" Conrad queried dryly.

"Of course he does. He's no more interested in marriage than I am. It's Johanna who's matchmaking. I didn't take it seriously, and I never imagined you would."

"It made me think you were more subtle than I'd thought. I wonder just how subtle you're being now."

"You'd see me more clearly if you'd stop looking for tricks and conspiracies," she said. "There aren't any. The key to me is that I'm a very simple, straightforward person."

"Oh, no!" Conrad said at once. "I would hardly describe you as simple and straightforward. Your effect on people is too powerful for that."

"If you mean Friederich . . ." she said haltingly.

"I don't only mean Friederich, as you very well know," he said, adding quickly, "You've also affected Horst."

So he was fencing with her, she thought. Very well. Two could play at that game. She leaned back and regarded him with a half-smile. "Don't worry about Friederich's heart," she told him lightly. "I'd never have taken risks with it if you yourself hadn't assured me it was safe to do so."

"I—?"

"Didn't you as good as warn me not to take him too seriously, because he fell in and out of love with such regularity?"

With a start of dismay, he remembered that it was true. He'd forgotten his own words, because he'd convinced himself that Friederich would act differently with this woman. A chill overtook him as he realized that Friederich's behavior was the same as always. The difference was in the woman he'd chosen this time. It was impossible to imagine anyone romancing her lightly and then passing on. The man who loved her would do so single-mindedly, deeply, passionately. He'd become hers, body and soul, oblivious to everything except her, counting the world well lost for her love, even if he only knew it for a brief, gleaming moment.

Now Conrad saw how dangerously close he'd drifted to the rocks. It took a considerable effort to force himself to shrug and say with a laugh, "You're quite right. I overreacted. You and Friederich are playing a lighthearted game." He looked directly at her. "Just as you and I did."

She was too proud to let him see that his answer disappointed her, so she just shrugged and said lightly, "You didn't say that this afternoon."

"But that's the whole point of a game," he retorted quickly. "Nothing you say counts next time." He shrugged. "So you can go back to flirting with my brother with a clear conscience."

Go back, after the glory of being held in Conrad's arms? Go back to her state of contented ignorance? No, that path was barred to her forever by the memory of his lips burning against hers and the passion in his voice as he murmured her name. From now on, she could only go forward to whatever heaven or hell might exist in this feeling that consumed her—but which Conrad wasn't yet prepared to recognize.

Not wanting her eyes to betray her, she turned to study the Lorelei rock, which reared up, glorious in the sunset. All around it, the beams of light slanted down the deep gorge into the river, like a shining ladder descending from the sky, and she had to shade her eyes to look right to the top. In the blinding dazzle, she could almost imagine she heard the sound of ethereal singing.

Conrad followed her gaze and his mouth twisted ironically. "It looks very romantic, doesn't it? The truth is far from romantic, but I suppose you wouldn't care for that. Too much reality."

"If romance is real, I don't think truth can destroy it," Laurel said quietly.

"But this romance isn't real. It's a fraud. Look—" He indicated the massive banks. "Just there, the gorge turns at a sharp angle, then turns again, so that every sound gives off a sevenfold echo. There are a dozen different currents making the water dangerous, and sharp rocks lurk under the surface. That's all it is. But fanciful folk prefer the pretty legend of the maiden, who sits on the rock singing sailors to their doom. There's no such thing as the Lorelei."

The force with which he said the final words impelled her to retort, "You don't mean that. You'd like to dismiss it, but in your heart I think you believe in her—and you fear her."

He drained his stein and set it down abruptly. "It's time we were going."

They didn't speak on the short journey home. As they entered the driveway, Laurel couldn't keep her thoughts from leaping forward to the moment when he would help her from the car, his big hands holding her against the warmth of his body.

With a sudden shock she realized that she was scheming. "Like a Victorian spinster," she mused, annoyed with herself. When he had stopped the car and reached out to help her, she spoke gruffly. "I can manage, thank you. I don't need help," she insisted.

But he ignored her, drawing her firmly from the car and holding her until she was steady. Looking up, she saw that his face was tense as if he was fighting an inner battle, and his dark eyes were aflame. For a moment he almost leaned forward and she felt his muscles harden. Then a shudder seemed to go through him, the moment passed, and she knew he'd won his struggle.

While Helga was helping Laurel to get ready for dinner that evening, there was a knock on the door. Helga answered and returned with a bouquet of pink roses and a large card. The card was hand-drawn and showed a stickman on his knees in a comically pleading pose. The caption began, If You Don't Forgive Me . . . and continued inside, My Heart Will Be Broken Forever, with another picture of the stickman pounding the floor in a paroxysm of grief.

She laughed out loud and Friederich appeared immediately.

"Don't try to fool me," she ordered severely. "Your heart's in fine condition."

"Of course," he agreed readily, "but it's polite to go through the motions. Seriously, do you forgive me?"

"I shouldn't, but I can't stay angry with someone who can make me laugh."

"I promise to back off. Conrad wasn't just being protective. He was ready to kill me for daring to touch you. I've never seen that look in his eyes before."

"You're imagining things," she said, trying to hide the little stab of pleasure his words gave her. "Don't tell Conrad what you're thinking. He wouldn't like it."

Friederich nodded. "My brilliant older brother isn't so brilliant about some things, is he?" he asked shrewdly. "He's always been like that. I don't know why, but I've never seen him really lose his head over a woman. Poor old fellow. To think what he misses!"

"He's probably taken warning from watching you," Laurel observed. "He's angry with me because he thinks you might be suffering from unrequited love. I told him he didn't need to worry about you."

"Hmmm. Unflattering, but accurate. Let me escort you to dinner so he can see that all's well between us."

It wasn't what she wanted, but there was no polite way to refuse, so she allowed him to take her arm and they went to the dining room together. Conrad's eyebrows rose, but he said nothing.

Horst arrived at the table wearing his monster mask. Johanna persuaded him that he'd eat better without it and he reluctantly laid it aside, but his streams of excited chatter didn't let up.

His happiness made Laurel smile with delight. She stole a glance at Conrad and caught his eyes on her. He looked away, but then turned back and met her gaze with a challenging one of his own, almost as though he was defying her to criticize him now. It was surely absurd to think he was asking for her approval, despite Horst's conviction that he had changed his mind because of her.

"Everybody dresses up for the carnival—" Horst was explaining to her.

"Not everybody," Conrad interrupted firmly. "Nothing will persuade me to dress up."

"But *you* will, won't you?" Horst begged Laurel.

"Certainly," she said promptly. "I shall go as someone with a bad leg."

Everybody laughed, and Johanna said, "I, too, shall dress sensibly. It will make a change from all those Brunnhildes and Siegfrieds. Nobody has any original ideas these days. When I was a child, people used to outdo each other trying to think of original costumes."

"Were there any good monsters?" Horst demanded eagerly.

"There were some excellent giants," Conrad told him, smiling.

"And didn't eight men band together to make a huge dragon, one year?" Laurel asked.

"I don't remember that," Friederich said.

"It was sixty years ago," Conrad told him. He looked at Laurel curiously. "How strange that you should know about that."

"I expect I read it somewhere," she said hastily. "I've been reading a lot of books from your library."

Conrad nodded and let the subject drop, but Laurel had the uncomfortable sensation of almost having fallen into a pit. It had been Anna who told her of the dragon, and she'd spoken without thinking. The rest of the meal was spent discussing the carnival, but once Laurel looked up to find Conrad's eyes on her, still fixed with the same curious expression.

When they left the table, Johanna watched as Laurel used her crutches to hop as far as the sofa. "You're already very skilled with those," she remarked. "Did you find it a strain going to the distillery?"

"It was very interesting," Laurel said, careful not to let her voice reveal any emotion, "and I didn't get at all tired."

Conrad had brought her coffee over himself. As he laid it on the table beside her, he said quietly, "But I believe there was a moment when you found your injury something of an impediment."

"I shall have to be more careful about getting into awkward situations," she said, matching his tone.

"I wonder how successfully you will manage that?" He moved away before she could reply.

The air seemed to be alive with electric currents. Friederich, either oblivious to the atmosphere or wanting to dispel it, fiddled with the record player and a moment later the room was filled with dance music. "Come along," he said, taking Laurel's hands. "Let's show them how well you can manage."

She tried to protest but he drew her firmly to her feet and guided her around the room in a waltz. His arm was strong around her waist. But there was only one man whose arms she wanted around her. Nevertheless, she forced herself to laugh and pretend to be having fun. Once, in turning, she found herself facing Conrad, and her heart leaped at the expression she saw in his eyes. It was the same fierce look that he'd had that afternoon, when he'd lashed out at his brother for daring to touch her. Seeing her in another man's arms made him burn with jealousy, but he wouldn't acknowledge it by so much as the flicker of a muscle.

Johanna sat smiling placidly at the sight of the two dancers. Then her glance fell on Conrad, and slowly her smile faded. She stared at him for a long time, but he stood lost in some trancelike vision that absorbed him, and never noticed her. Johanna followed the line of his gaze, and her eyes narrowed.

The door opened and Helga came in, going straight to Conrad. She had to speak twice before she could get his attention, but when she did, he nodded and went swiftly out of the room.

"I hope that doesn't mean grandfather is worse," Johanna said worriedly.

"Oh, no," Helga assured her. "He just wants to talk."

"That's as much dancing as I can manage," Laurel told Friederich firmly. The incident had given her a jolt, reminding her that she still hadn't kept her promise to Anna. She didn't know much much time might be left.

Conrad slipped quietly into his grandfather's room and approached the bed where the old man lay propped up against pillows. His eyes were closed, and for a moment Conrad watched him sadly, seeing how frail he was. The old, lean face was full of weariness, yet something kept him clinging to life.

Baron Kaspar von Feldstein opened his eyes and smiled warmly at his grandson. "You sent for me," Conrad reminded him. "What can I do for you, grandfather?"

"Sit by me awhile." His voice was so faint a thread that Conrad had to draw his chair close to the bed and lean forward. He took the baron's hand between his own muscular, capable ones, noticing that it, too, was large, although wasted now. And he realized that this old man had once been young and vigorous, in a long-ago world that had glowed with springtime.

"I want you to do something for me," Kaspar said slowly, after a while.

"Anything."

"You won't like it, I'm afraid."

"That doesn't matter. Whatever it is, I'll do it."

"The picture of the Lorelei...I want it up here, where I can see it." He felt the faint pressure as Conrad's hand tightened. "I knew you'd disapprove."

"I just wish I understood—but no matter. I'll arrange it."

"I, too, wish you understood," Kaspar sighed. "But it's a mystery that can't be explained. Perhaps one day you'll discover it for yourself. I hope so."

"I do very well without mysteries," Conrad said uneasily.

Kaspar smiled, as if pitying him. "I, too, thought so once."

"What put this into your head now?"

"My dreams. I have them constantly. *She* seemed to come back to me, and all was well. I've had that dream before, but when I awoke it wasn't true. Now—it's strange, but I seem to feel her near me."

For a moment his face bore the look of a young man, brilliant with joy at his beloved's nearness. Conrad stared. "You speak as if you still loved her," he whispered.

"I have loved her all my life. I shall love her until my last moment, and beyond," Kaspar said simply.

"But she broke your heart. She deserted you." The words were a cry of protest.

"I shouldn't have let her desert me. I tried to find her, but I gave up in despair. I was wrong to give up. I know that now. I should have searched to the ends of the earth, and when I found her, I should have demanded that she tell me to my face that she didn't love me, that she had never loved me, and that everything between us had been a mockery. I don't believe she could have spoken those words."

Conrad was startled by the intensity that possessed his grandfather's frail form. Power seemed to flow from him, communicating itself to Conrad through the thin hand he held. Abruptly he rose and began to stride about the room, trying to use movement to exorcise the storm of unfamiliar feelings that troubled him. Kaspar's words had shaken him to the core. How could this man, whom he had always admired, speak of chasing after a woman and begging her to return to him?

He saw Kaspar looking at him out of shadowed eyes, and quickly returned his attention to the bedside. "My greatest fear has always been for you," his grandfather said. "You remind me of my father. He was a great man, but a very rigid one. His life was ruled by pride, and I don't think he ever knew any joy. Not that he thought personal feelings mattered much."

"I hope I'm not that extreme," Conrad said, trying to speak lightly, "but I believe a man should keep his pride. Without it, what does he have?"

"He might have love," Kaspar said gently. "Pride has been the curse of our family. One day, perhaps, your happiness may depend on a woman's love. Don't let it slip away, as I did."

"My happiness will never depend on a woman," Conrad said firmly.

Kaspar spoke as if the last strength had suddenly drained out of him. "Then God help you!" he said wearily, "for your life will be empty."

A strange feeling possessed Conrad. As Kaspar spoke, he seemed to hear Laurel's voice saying, as she had said a few days ago, "I pity you because you know nothing." Of course, he reasoned, the similarity between her words and those of his grandfather was a mere coincidence, but it was almost as though the minds of the old man and the young woman mirrored each other. Quickly he shied away from that alarming thought.

He asked harshly, "And you? Did your love give you lifelong happiness?"

"Love doesn't promise that," Kaspar declared, almost sternly. "It gives you a moment of glory, and perhaps there will be many more, perhaps only one to last forever. But the one moment is enough, and nothing is ever the same afterward. The failure was mine... all mine...."

He closed his eyes again. Conrad stayed until he was sure his grandfather was asleep, then quietly rose and went to the window, leaning out into the warm night air. From far below came hollow sounds that were caught up in the swirling air currents of the gorge, echoing repeatedly until they faded into silence. In the darkness they had an eerie, yearning quality. A fanciful man might almost begin to believe the legends, he told himself. But it was only an echo. Nothing more. *Nothing more.*

He discovered that he was breathing hard and his knuckles had turned white where he gripped the windowsill. His heart was beating strongly, as if with alarm. He thrust the thought roughly away and wondered why he was falling prey to delusions tonight.

He'd asked his grandfather that last bitter question out of rage at the woman who had left him with only a husk of a life. Now his thoughts turned uneasily to another woman, one who had insinuated herself into his home and threatened his peace of mind. His grandfather was proof of the terrible devastation love could bring a man, and Conrad would never allow himself to risk his own fate. But still . . . Laurel unsettled him as no woman ever had. She could make him behave illogically, finding excuses to keep her here and seek her out, instead of sending her packing. She was in his thoughts more often than she had any business to be.

Recently he'd come to have an incredible suspicion about her. His grandfather's words, "I seem to feel her near me," had made him uneasy. If what he suspected was true, it was yet another reason for keeping her away from Kaspar.

He returned to the bed and stood looking down at the exhausted old man, seeing the lines of suffering on his face. Now that he was unobserved, he allowed himself a gentle expression. All the love his strong, protective nature was capable of was in his voice as he said softly, "You're going to have peace. Nothing—and no one—is going to trouble you. I promise you that."

Kaspar gave no sign of hearing him, and after a moment Conrad quietly left the room.

The next morning, he summoned Friederich to help him move the picture. "You took enough time getting here," he said when Friederich finally appeared in the anteroom.

"I was upstairs, visiting the old man."

Conrad looked at him sharply. "Alone, I hope."

"Yes, don't worry. You made yourself very plain on that subject." He looked up at the painted face of the Lorelei, with its half-smile that seemed to encompass

GET YOUR GIFTS FROM SILHOUETTE®
ABSOLUTELY FREE!

Mail this card today!

PLACE
JOKER
STICKER
HERE

PLAY THIS CARD RIGHT!

YES! Please send me my 4 Silhouette Romance™ novels FREE along with my free Gold-Plated Chain and free mystery gift. I wish to receive all the benefits of the Silhouette Reader Service™ as explained on the opposite page.

(U-SIL-R-11/90) 215 CIS HAYW

NAME _____
(PLEASE PRINT)

ADDRESS _____ APT. ____

CITY _____

STATE _____ ZIP CODE _____

Offer limited to one per household and not valid to current Silhouette Romance subscribers. All orders subject to approval.

SILHOUETTE READER SERVICE
"NO RISK" GUARANTEE

- There's no obligation to buy—and the free books remain yours to keep.
- You don't pay for postage and handling and receive books before they appear in stores.
- You may end your subscription anytime—just write and let us know or return any shipment to us at our cost.

IT'S NO JOKE!

MAIL THE POSTPAID CARD AND
GET FREE GIFTS AND $9.00 WORTH OF
SILHOUETTE NOVELS—FREE!

If offer card is missing, write to:
Silhouette Reader Service, P.O. Box 1867, Buffalo, NY 14269-1867

them both. "You know, Horst is right," he said thoughtfully. "It is like her."

"Then take warning," Conrad said shortly. "Don't become even more her victim than you already have been."

"Am I a victim?" Friederich asked quizzically. "It doesn't feel like it."

"Didn't she lead you on so that you'd fall in love with her? And all the time she was using you. When she discovered you wouldn't do what she wanted, what happened?"

Friederich grinned. "I got my face slapped. Well, it's not the first time that's happened, and I suppose I was asking for it. As you saw, I made my peace with Laurel last night. We're the best of friends now. The only one who's really disappointed is Johanna. She'd practically arranged the wedding date."

"Are you telling me you weren't serious?" Conrad asked slowly.

Friederich shrugged. "No more than I ever am. You know me. She brightened up a dull summer. I was famished for entertainment."

"And that's your idea of entertainment—playing with a woman's feelings? Suppose she'd taken you seriously?"

Friederich gave him a strange look. "You've misunderstood, dear brother. The Lorelei never took me seriously. We both knew the rules, even if you didn't. The entertainment I referred to was the sight of you, on hot coals for her, and trying to pretend you weren't."

Conrad paled, but managed to speak in a steady voice. "I believe you've taken leave of your senses," he said coldly. "I assure you, I'm in no danger."

Friederich gave an impish glance up at the boatman in the painting. "I imagine he was thinking the same thing just before he went under. Why did you send for me, by the way?"

"It doesn't matter," Conrad said, ushering him out of the room. "I've changed my mind."

Later that day, he called a servant to help move the picture.

Chapter Seven

On the evening of the carnival, Laurel realized how much she'd been looking forward to getting out again. Her balance had greatly improved, and tonight she decided to discard her crutches and rely on a cane.

Luckily she'd brought with her the only expensive clothes she possessed: a long evening dress of blue-green silk and a floor-length black velvet opera cloak with a hood. The cloak had been Anna's last gift, and she'd bought it despite Laurel's protests that it was "too dramatic".

"At your age, you can afford to be dramatic," Anna had insisted, and now Laurel was glad of the beautiful garment, which covered her plaster leg and made her look less ungainly. The dress swirled softly around her, and its hint of green brought out the same tinge in the blue of her eyes. Her hair flowed free.

Conrad, Horst and Johanna were waiting for her in the hall, Horst was in full "monster" costume, skipping impatiently as he waited to leave. He beamed when he saw Laurel. "Do I look all right?" she asked teasingly.

"Just right," he said happily.

Conrad was conservatively dressed in a dinner jacket and black bow tie. He took the long cloak and draped it around her shoulders, leaning close so that he could speak into her ear without the others overhearing. "Did you deliberately choose that look?" he asked softly.

"What look?"

"Don't play games. You know who you look like." He added provocatively, "the Lorelei."

"I wore these clothes because they're my only good ones," she assured him. "I wasn't trying to look like anyone special."

"You don't have to try," he murmured. "You are . . . who you are. You couldn't be anyone else."

"I never thought I'd hear you talking like that," she whispered back.

"I accept it. That doesn't mean I'm happy about it." Abruptly, Conrad stepped away from her and raised his voice. "Horst will go in the first car with Friederich and Boris, and we three will follow separately."

"I'm sure Friederich and Laurel would like to be together," Johanna said with a bright, determined smile.

"Please don't change the arrangements on our account," Laurel said hastily.

"Let's go," Conrad said, ushering them out. While he delivered Horst into Friederich's care, Johanna opened the rear door of the second car. "I hate sitting in the front seat," she said, "but I'll gladly do so for your sake. You'll have more room in the back."

In fact, the back was rather cramped, and Laurel would have managed more easily in the front. But she didn't want an argument, so she made the best of it, while Johanna settled herself beside Conrad.

Dusk was falling and they could see the brilliant lights of Hargen as they descended the steep road. Conrad drove into the town, set the two women down, and promised to be back once he'd parked the car. While they waited, Johanna insisted on going to a nearby café and buying Laurel an ice cream. "We can sit at an outside table so that Conrad can see us when he returns," she said.

Laurel could sense something different in the older woman's manner. Although still apparently friendly, she seemed strained. But her next remark seemed to explain it. "I'm always nervous in large crowds," she said, moving her chair slightly to let someone squeeze past. "They jostle so. Since my husband's death, I've been reluctant to go out more than necessary."

"Perhaps you should go out more. You're still young and—"

"Please." Johanna held up her hand. "Don't say I can marry again. I don't want to. Horst is my life, and he's happy in Feldstein Castle. It's where he belongs. One day—" She broke off with an awkward laugh, then resumed quickly. "I expect you, too, are uneasy among all these people. It must make it so hard to walk with a cane."

"I'm improving fast," Laurel assured her. "If I collide with people, it usually hurts them more than me," she added with a chuckle.

Johanna's humorless face didn't relax into a smile. "I think your attitude is very brave," she said. "But you'll be glad to know that we always have reserved seats in the stands—in the front row, of course."

"Why, 'of course'?" Laurel asked innocently.

Johanna seemed a little shocked. "The von Feldsteins are aristocrats. As the most important family in the district, they naturally have the place of honor. Conrad would be very displeased if any attention were forgotten."

"I wonder if he really would," Laurel mused. She found it hard to imagine Conrad minding whether his neighbors showed him elaborate deference or not. "Surely he's too practical to care about such things."

"Certainly he's practical, but that doesn't mean he cares nothing for family pride. Conrad knows who he is and he expects other people to know, too."

"Yet only the other night, you were telling me that the family moves with the times," Laurel reminded her.

"I was speaking of Friederich's marriage, a very different matter if you'll forgive my saying so. Conrad will soon be the baron. If he ever contemplated marriage, not that there is any sign of it, he would be forced to take a more—let's say *traditional* view."

She stared hard at Laurel, but the effect was lost. Laurel had noticed Conrad coming back through the crowd and was waving to attract his attention. He dwarfed every other man there, she thought, and in her glow of happiness, she entirely missed Johanna's final words.

"The stand isn't far from here," Conrad said, helping Laurel to her feet and giving her his arm for the short distance. When they reached the stand, he helped her up the wooden steps, showed her to a seat in the front row, and sat beside her before Johanna could object. "We have a good view from here," he remarked. "Unfortunately, everyone else gets a good look at us."

"You don't like being looked at?" Laurel asked.

"I'd be happier without all the attention. It's even worse when we eat. We have to sit at the mayor's table, which is on a raised dais, and it makes me feel like a monkey having tea in front of a crowd in the zoo."

Laurel laughed out loud, but Johanna was stiff with disapproval. "It's one of the penalties of your position," she reminded her brother-in-law.

Conrad smiled at her. "Yes, Johanna," he said, kindly but with resignation, as if they'd covered this ground many times before.

The stand behind them was almost full, and an expectant buzz rose all around them. Then the sound of music could be heard in the distance, and the next moment there was a cheer as the head of the procession appeared around the corner.

First came the town band, puffing enthusiastically on their brass instruments. Then came the floats, each bearing characters from the Rhine's colorful history. Hans, the blind archer, shot an arrow into the throat of his tormentor, Siebold. The bride, Elisabeth, recoiled in horror as the priest revealed her bridegroom as the devil in disguise. Knights in gleaming armor struck noble poses, magicians cast smoky spells, and beautiful maidens struggled with huge snakes, all to the accompaniment of cheers from the crowd.

Laurel watched, entranced, as the Rhine legends that had filled her dreams since childhood paraded before her eyes. Once, Anna had walked through these very streets, her hand clasped in the hand of the man she loved. She seemed to be very close now. Thinking herself unobserved, Laurel closed her eyes and made a silent promise to Anna that she wouldn't fail her. When she opened them, Conrad was looking at her. "Are you all right?" he enquired.

"I'm fine," she said quickly. "I was just...thinking of something."

"Something that takes you away into your own secret world. Now I know I must stay on my guard."

He'd leaned closer to speak into her ear. Laurel turned her head slightly to say, "I've never seen you off guard."

The crowd's roar drowned out his reply, but she watched his mouth shape the words, "That isn't true. You know it isn't—*don't you?*"

"Yes," she said. His lips were barely apart, but she could hear the slight rasping of his breath.

"Oh, look!" Johanna said excitedly. "There's Horst!"

Conrad seemed to surface from a dream, and drew back from Laurel sharply. Laurel felt the world stop spinning and settle into place once again. She forced her attention away from him, focusing instead on the children who had appeared next in the procession. There were fifty youngsters pretending to be dwarfs, hobgoblins and fairies, hopping excitedly and waving to the crowd. Horst's face was hidden, but Laurel recognized his monster costume. Two giants walked near him, one tall and slim, one squat and broad shouldered, both sporting wrinkled tights and blond wigs, and carrying mighty clubs. They roared and took mock-ferocious swings at the delighted crowd, but beneath the clowning, Friederich and Boris were keeping close watch over Horst.

Behind them came a cluster of adults in their own choice of fancy dress. As Johanna had said, there were

any number of Brunnhildes and Siegfrieds, and an ar-
ray of Rhine maidens. Another band followed, and
then the last float of all, and the biggest. It was built
very high to represent a tall rock, and on the pinnacle
sat a young woman dressed as the Lorelei, running a
golden comb through her long blond hair. At the bottom was a tiny boat in which a man crouched, staring
yearningly upward at her. A huge cheer burst from the
crowd, and they clapped and roared their approval.

Jangling and swaying, the procession made its way
to the town square, where the floats diverted, coming
to rest in the side streets.

"Now we have to make our way to the square,"
Conrad said to Laurel. "Luckily, it's only a short
walk."

She took his arm and along with Johanna, they
mingled with the excited crowd surging through the
streets in the direction of the square. When they
reached their destination, Laurel exclaimed aloud with
delight and Conrad smiled back at her. It was dark
now, and the trees had been hung with colored lan-
terns, which lit up the cobblestones below and struck
gleams off the gilt hands of the town hall clock. Tres-
tle tables had been set up around the square, their
snowy white cloths already bearing plates for the venison that would be washed down with beer from tall
steins.

Conrad's eyes flickered over the crowd until he saw
Friederich making his way toward them, Horst's hand
clutched firmly in his, Boris in the background. He and
Johanna relaxed, and Laurel experienced a moment of
intense relief. If anything had happened to Horst, she
would have felt responsible.

As Conrad had said, they were seated at the mayor's table on a raised dais. As he took his place beside the mayor, Johanna quickly slipped into the seat beside him, calling, "Horst, you sit next to me, then Friederich. Laurel, you'll have more room at the end."

The end seat was at a right angle to the others, making it easier for Laurel to find somewhere for her cane. Horst was running around the table, chattering nineteen to the dozen. He'd clearly had a wonderful time, and Johanna's efforts to get him to sit down fell on deaf ears. With an indulgent smile, Conrad listened to him for a few moments, then pointed firmly to his seat.

Friederich gave Laurel a wide grin, showing two teeth that had been blacked out for effect. "You look absolutely horrible," she informed him with a smile.

"Thank you," he said, accurately judging her comment to be a compliment. "You look glorious." His eyes ran over her admiringly. "I think I shall fall desperately in love with you all over again."

"No, don't do that," she teased. "It's boring to repeat yourself."

"True." He sighed, then brightened. "You should have seen Conrad's face when I told him I wasn't brokenhearted. He couldn't decide whether to be indignant for your sake or delighted for mine—not to mention his own. I haven't enjoyed myself so much in years."

Horst's reappearance between them saved Laurel from having to reply to this.

Johanna pleaded with her son to behave, but it was Laurel's comment, "If you don't sit down you'll miss the food," that sent him back to his seat.

They ate venison under the stars while the local acrobatic club entertained them with an old-fashioned tumbling act. Then speeches were made and toasts drunk with Feldstein brandy, which Conrad had donated for the occasion. He looked uncomfortable while his generosity was being praised and a special toast drunk in his honor.

"Here, here," Friederich called enthusiastically. "Hey, what's the matter?" He'd noticed Laurel trying to look under the table.

"My cane has slipped down," she said.

"I'll get it." He retrieved it and returned it to her, at the same time seizing her hand and giving it a gallant kiss before she could snatch it away.

"That's enough," she said.

"Sorry. I just can't resist getting Conrad's goat."

"Nonsense, he doesn't care what I do," she insisted, but inwardly she was eager to hear it denied.

"Doesn't care? Look at the way he's glowering at us, but pretending not to. He'd like to kick my behind. I think you've finally achieved the miracle that women have failed at accomplishing for years—the capture of my impossible brother. What do you think, Johanna?"

"I think you're talking a lot of nonsense," Johanna said frostily. She leaned across Friederich to Laurel. "Please excuse him. His tongue runs away with him, but I'm sure you're too sensible to take his fantasies seriously."

"I promise you I know what to take seriously, and what not to," Laurel said ambiguously, which made Johanna give her a sharp look.

At last the speeches were over. A sigh went through the crowd as the sound of an accordion filled the air, playing the song all Rhinelanders knew and loved— "The Song of the Lorelei." In seconds, they were all singing the words as the Lorelei float appeared again, bearing the buxom young woman to receive homage.

Laurel turned so that she faced the float, one arm resting lightly on the table. From where Conrad sat, only her profile was visible, the angle of her head revealing the clean, beautiful length of her throat in the magic light of the lamps. She was singing with the others, and, as he realized that she knew all the words of the song, the incredible suspicion that had grown in him of late was confirmed. He clenched his hands until the nails dug into his palms. Somehow, tonight he must find the strength to tell her to go. In the morning, she must leave the castle forever.

Suddenly, he was desperate to get away from here. He was offended by the blowsy, painted creature on the float, with her utter lack of mystery. There was no subtlety in the toothy smile with which she acknowledged the crowd's tribute, no beauty in the coarse fibers of her yellow wig, no magic in her glances.

The true Lorelei had silky tresses that streamed down her slim body like an endless river of gold; her voice was soft and her smile an enticement. She could make a man flout his own deepest convictions and never regret it.

The song ended and the float was drawn away. The accordions played on, and gradually dancers drifted into the center of the square and clasped each other, swaying to the waltz. "Let's dance and make Conrad really mad," Friederich urged.

"Thank you, but no," Laurel said firmly. "Besides, we've got to keep an eye on Horst."

"Horst is dancing," Friederich said. "Look."

Laurel followed his pointing finger and chuckled to see that Horst had indeed found himself a dancing partner, a little girl dressed as a witch, who was giving him instructions with every step.

"So it's a positive duty to dance," Friederich pleaded.

"Indeed it is," said Conrad's voice behind them. Looking up, Laurel saw his hand extended to her, and a look in his eyes that brooked no refusal. A wave of relief swept over her. She reached up and Conrad clasped her hands and drew her to her feet.

Couples made way for them as they moved into the center of the square, where the light from the colored lamps was dimmest and full of shadows. Conrad held her tightly against him, steadying her with an arm around her waist. "Is this too difficult for your leg?" he asked. "Do you want to sit down?"

"No," she told him. "I want to be here." She knew the intensity in her voice must have revealed something of her heart's turmoil, but she couldn't stop to think about that. She was in his arms again, where she'd longed to be ever since that other time, when he'd held her with baffled rage, unable to resist her, or his own feelings. This time there was a different look in his eyes, and the strong hands on her body held a new message, but what it was or might become she had yet to learn.

Conrad knew he shouldn't be doing this. Etiquette demanded that he dance first with the wives of local dignitaries, and by singling this woman out, he was proclaiming to the world that she had a hold over him. He was vaguely aware of knowing glances from the crowd, but he was past caring. In the last few days, he'd run the gamut of emotions from anger to torment, from resolution to helpless yearning. Now he was with her again, and nothing else mattered.

He tightened his arms quickly as he felt her stumble against another couple. "I'm afraid I'm rather clumsy," she said.

"The floor's too crowded for you. Let's go closer to the side," he suggested, leading her away from the center and toward a small gap in the side tables that lined the square. They squeezed through, and suddenly they were out of the square altogether, and in a darkened side street, where the lights barely reached and the music was faint. "We'll have more room here," he said, taking her into his arms again and beginning to dance.

He moved gracefully and slowly, fitting his steps to her hesitant movements, and suddenly she found it easy. She forgot about her leg. Everything faded and there was only the two of them, alone together in the scented night air, under the stars.

Now, he thought. Now was the moment to do as he'd resolved, to tell her that she must leave his house and go far away where she could no longer trouble him. Instead, he drew her into a shadowed doorway, where no one could see them, bent his head and laid his mouth on hers. "Lorelei..." he murmured against her lips. "Lorelei . . . never leave me . . ."

"Never," she whispered, dazed with wonder at the feelings that were coursing through her. "Never as long as you want me."

She thought she heard him say, "Always," but he was kissing her again and her thoughts were whirling faster and faster until they ceased being thoughts at all and became fused with the sensations his lips were evoking. She wanted it to go on forever, but already, to her dismay, the outside world was intruding. She thought she heard a faint scream, and then the sounds of a commotion that seemed to come from a long way off.

Conrad lifted his head and stood listening for a moment. The scream came again, and this time there was no mistaking the voice. It was Johanna's, and she was calling Horst.

"Oh, no!" Laurel exclaimed in horror.

They hurried back to the square, which was only a few feet away, although it had seemed like another world only a moment ago. Johanna was rushing hither and thither, frantically calling Horst's name, but there was no sign of the child. "He's gone," she wept as Conrad reached her.

"Who saw him last?" Conrad demanded. "Friederich, you were supposed to be watching him." He spoke sharply to cover the dreadful gnawing of guilt inside him.

"I *was* watching him," Friederich protested. "He was under my eye all the time, but suddenly he just— vanished."

"They snatched him," Johanna cried.

"I don't think so," Laurel said. "I'm pretty sure he's just escaped like he did last time."

"Of course you'd think so," Johanna flashed. "You don't want to admit that this is all your fault—"

"Johanna, please," Conrad said quickly. "That won't help us."

"And you," Johanna snapped. "At one time you'd never have taken your eyes off him in a crowd. But now that woman is here, and you have eyes for no one else. You used to be so cautious and sensible, but now you don't even see what's happened. *The Lorelei has bewitched you.*"

For a long moment, they all seemed to stand petrified like figures on a frieze. Then Conrad's eyes, full of shock, rested on Laurel. Even in the dim glow of the fairy lamps, she could see that his face drained of color as he recognized the truth. A tremor wracked him.

Then he recovered himself. "Where's Boris?" he asked, in an unsteady voice.

"He went off looking," Friederich told him.

Just then, Boris appeared from the inside of a shop and spread his hands to show Conrad that he'd found nothing. His expression was anguished.

Laurel turned to Friederich. "Was Horst still dancing with that little girl?" she asked.

"Yes, they seemed to have struck up a friendship. Come to think of it, she's vanished too."

"No, she hasn't," Laurel said excitedly. She had been looking around the square, and her sharp eyes had noted something. "I saw her a moment ago, sneaking some little cakes from a table over there." She pointed. "Horst hasn't been kidnapped. They've just gone off together to have an adventure, and if we're quick she'll lead us to him."

Conrad hurried to the place she had indicated, but the little girl had vanished. He was confronted by a short street that led to the river. The gleam of water could just be seen at the far end.

"I can hear music," Laurel remarked.

"That'll be the gypsies," Friederich said. "They always park their caravans on that patch of land during carnival." Suddenly, his face lit up. "Of course! Why didn't we think of it? *Gypsies*. Children love them."

"Come on, then," Conrad said tensely. He led the way, with the others hurrying after him.

Laurel's heart was thumping. If Horst turned up safely, everything might still be all right. But if anything had happened to him, Conrad would never forgive himself—or her. His suspicions would take over again, and she would lose—for Anna, and for herself.

The road ended in a rough patch of open ground next to the water, where a dozen brightly colored gypsy caravans were parked in a circle. At the center, several couples were doing a traditional dance to the accompaniment of scratchy violins. A few looked like gypsies, but many were townsfolk in fancy dress. And there among them, bouncing about enthusiastically, were Horst and the little girl.

Johanna gave a shriek of joy and raced across to Horst, her arms open. He sighed with resignation, and although he allowed himself to be enveloped in a maternal embrace, it was clear he felt his fun had been unreasonably spoiled. But he looked apprehensive as Conrad approached.

"You'd better have a good explanation for running away this time," Conrad growled.

"I didn't exactly run away," Horst explained carefully. "At least—I meant to come back." He took the girl's hand. "This is Ella. She's my friend."

"It was my fault," Ella said robustly. "I said I'd take Horst to visit the gypsies because he'd never seen any. He's never done *anything*," she added with youthful scorn.

Horst flung her a dark look, and a scuffle might have developed if Conrad hadn't said quickly, "Never mind that. At least you're both safe."

Behind them the dance was still going on, but one of the couples stopped and came over. The woman was tall, buxom and jolly, sporting long, artificial plaits and a winged helmet. The man was short and squat, and puffed uncomfortably inside clanking armor. They introduced themselves as Ella's parents, Thora and Otto Kaufmann. "You've probably seen our bakery," Thora said. "It's the big one in the town square."

"Yes, I know it," Johanna said stiffly. "I often have some of your cakes delivered to the castle."

The Kaufmanns became a little shy as they learned the identity of Ella's playmate, but Conrad dispelled any awkwardness. "Now that the children are friends," he said, smiling, "I hope Ella will come and play with Horst." In response to a frantic whisper from Horst, he added, "and bring her two brothers."

Horst bounced about with joy, and Laurel smiled at his pleasure. Only Johanna didn't seem pleased. She was glaring coldly at Laurel.

"Why did you do that?" she demanded of Conrad when Ella and her parents had gone. "They are bakers."

"Good. They'll open windows for Horst," Conrad said mildly, "especially that little girl. You heard what she said. He's never done anything, and that's our fault—or rather, it's mine. Luckily, we have a chance to put things right." He looked at Horst. "But if you ever vanish like that and worry your mother again, I'll make you sorry you were born. Understood?"

"Yes, Uncle," Horst said, with a not very convincing imitation of meekness.

"I'm taking you right home," Johanna declared.

Conrad nodded. "It's time he was in bed. Friederich—"

"I think I'll stay," Friederich said, sliding away. "There's a lot of charming company here tonight." He vanished into the throng.

Boris appeared with the car, which he'd slipped away to fetch. Johanna climbed in after Horst, then pointedly looked at Laurel. But she stayed where she was, feeling Conrad's hand on her arm detaining her. Johanna's mouth tightened and she slammed the door. Boris started up the engine, and a moment later the car had gone.

Laurel turned to Conrad. Now that there was no need to keep up a front, his face was ghastly with the nightmare of what might have happened. Pity stabbed her, and without a word she put her arms around him.

Chapter Eight

Conrad felt drained by the evening's events. He was only partly aware of Laurel until she enfolded him in her arms, her face full of pity and understanding. "It's been a terrible night for you, hasn't it?" she said gently.

He couldn't speak. The reassurance of her clasp was sweet, and he tightened his fingers around hers. He had the strange sensation that only her strength was keeping him on his feet.

"Let's get away from this noise," she suggested.

He nodded and let her lead him away. "Take the next street," he said suddenly. "It's quiet, and a friend of mine has a place that will still be open."

They found the little restaurant, open as he'd said, but almost deserted. The sleepy, elderly waiter smiled and unfolded himself from the stool where he'd been dozing and motioned to them to take any table they wanted. They took one in a secluded corner, away from the door. The waiter put a bottle of white wine on the table and then, in response to a murmur from Laurel, set a whisky and soda in front of Conrad.

He looked briefly surprised, then downed it quickly. "I guess I don't have to ask how you knew I needed that," he said.

"You always have one after dinner," she explained, "and your face was a ghastly color."

"The feeling inside me is worse. For a moment, I thought I could hear Markus's voice, begging me to care for his loved ones. I thought I'd failed again...." He was wracked by an uncontrollable shudder. Once it had passed, he looked at her out of haunted eyes. "Johanna was right. I forgot everything else. Was that what you wanted, to make me your fool?"

"If you're a fool, so am I," she said softly. "I forgot everything else too."

He held her hands in a grip of iron. "If you're lying," he said hoarsely, "may you never be forgiven."

"Do you believe I'm lying?" she asked.

"I don't know. God help me, I don't know."

"Why are you afraid of me?" she asked urgently.

"It's myself I fear, more than you. I thought I was safe, but you showed me I'm not. You bring magic with you, but it's the most dangerous magic in the world. Horst saw it before I did. The day you came, he said you were the Lorelei. I denied it, although my heart knew it was true. All my life, the Lorelei has haunted me. I knew I must confront her one day, but when the time came I was still taken by surprise."

She ran her fingertips gently down his cheek and felt him tremble. "But why deny it?" she asked softly. "Suppose I *am* the Lorelei—what then?"

"Then I ought to block my ears and flee from your spell. But I can't do it, any more than the other poor fools you've enticed to their destruction through the ages."

"Conrad, please…you're talking wildly. You don't really believe any of this."

"Don't I? Let me tell you something. I know a man who listened to the Lorelei's song and was lured to his doom. He didn't drown when she deserted him, but it might have been better for him if he had. He lived on. He even seemed to recover, he married and everyone thought he was happy. But his wife knew otherwise. She knew she'd married a husk of a man whose heart was given to the Lorelei. He's old now, but her ghost still haunts him."

Laurel's heart began to beat with excitement. "You mean your grandfather, don't you?"

"Yes. It happened nearly sixty years ago. He was in his twenties and he fell in love with a local girl called Anna Morgan. She became everything to him—his love, his world, his future wife and mother of his children. She said she loved him, and he believed her. But three days before the wedding she vanished, leaving nothing behind. He went to her home, but her landlord said she'd gone without leaving an address. She'd left nothing for him, not a letter, not a word, nothing.

"He was devastated. He managed to discover that she'd bought a ticket for a steamer traveling upriver, but he couldn't find out where it had docked. He traveled the river for weeks, getting off at every stop, asking people if they'd seen her. He went without food, without sleep, until he became disheveled and wild-eyed, and people used to speak of the madman who spent his life searching for a woman who didn't exist." Conrad clenched his hands tightly. "They jeered at him, and drew their children aside protectively."

Laurel felt a sudden pricking in her eyes at the picture of the young man, wandering in a hellish wilderness, endlessly seeking the woman he'd loved and lost. "How terrible," she said, her voice resonant with pity.

He shot her a sharp glance, as if wondering whether he could trust her pity. "Yes, it was terrible," he agreed. "I heard it from his sister many years later. She was the one who brought him home and cared for him. He'd contracted pneumonia and it nearly killed him. In his fever he raved deliriously about the Lorelei until they were afraid that, even if he lived, he would never be rational again.

"In the end, his body recovered, and his mind seemed to do the same. He talked sensibly, but the spirit had gone out of him. His sister invited their distant cousin, Dorothea, to visit and worked hard to promote a match between them. I think he married Dorothea because he didn't have the energy to argue about it. Poor woman. She knew whom he really loved, and how little of him belonged to her.

"My grandfather never got over Anna. He gave her photograph to an artist and told him to paint the Lorelei with her face. When I was a child, I once found him standing in front of that picture with a terrible look in his eyes. He told me about her, probably thinking I was too young to understand. But I learned of the destructiveness of love before I learned anything else about it. Since then, if I think I hear the siren song, I take care to steer well away."

"But perhaps he thinks his suffering was worth the love he once had," Laurel suggested eagerly. "Perhaps he knows that, despite everything, she really loved him.''

"Never," Conrad said vehemently. "She broke his heart."

"But she also broke her own heart. I don't know why she left him, but . . ." Laurel hesitated before saying, "I know she loved him all her life."

Conrad gave her a curious look. "How do you know this?"

She took a deep breath. "Because Anna Morgan was my grandmother."

For a long moment Conrad didn't move. He seemed to be searching her face. Then he nodded. "I suspected as much," he said heavily. "I've tried to tell myself that I was imagining things, that no kin of Anna Morgan would dare come here, where she'd caused so much grief. But you have her face, the face in the painting."

"Yes, I believe I look very much like her when she was young."

"So much so that it's alarming. And when I heard you speak German with the accent of a Rhinelander, I knew you must have roots in these parts."

"And I slipped up by mentioning the dragon, didn't I? I've known about the carnival virtually all my life. It's been so much a part of my own history that I forgot I'd learned it from my grandmother."

Conrad's eyes kindled. "She talked to you about her youth?"

"She talked a great deal about it. I loved listening to her. She made the Rhine sound like the most wonderful place in the world, full of mystery and beauty—a place where the impossible could come true."

As she spoke, her voice softened and her eyes grew bright. Conrad saw it, and a host of confused feelings took over within him. It was as though he looked through Kaspar's eyes, and saw the woman that *he* had seen, and she was irresistible.

Then anger washed over him, and he said bitterly, "If she told you so much, perhaps she also let you into the secret of why she smashed my grandfather to pieces on the rocks of her cruelty and indifference?"

"She wasn't cruel or indifferent," Laurel exclaimed, stung into indignation by this slander of Anna. "She loved him."

"Loved him so much that she deserted him just before their wedding, without a reason, without even seeing him face-to-face, without doing anything that might have made it easier for him. Don't pretend that wasn't cruel."

"She—might have been forced to do it that way," Laurel said hesitantly.

"Why?"

She made a helpless gesture. "I don't know."

Conrad gave a hard, mirthless laugh. "And yet you say she confided in you."

"She told me *some* things, but not everything. Whenever she spoke of love, it was with a special poignant note in her voice, as though she'd had some shattering experience that had marked her for life, but which had been so beautiful that she could never regret it. It made me think—" she stopped and blushed as she saw Conrad's eyes on her.

"Yes? What did it make you think?"

"That it must be wonderful to know that feeling," she said wistfully. "I promised myself that I'd never settle for anything less, no matter how long I had to wait.''

He shook his head. ''You're chasing fantasies. You'll wait forever for that dream to become reality.''

''No,'' she said softly, ''not forever.'' She wasn't sure if Conrad heard her.

He did, and his heart leaped at what he thought was her meaning. The enigmatic smile on her face tempted him. He wanted her to say more, but he knew that the more she said, the greater his danger. ''Our respective grandparents seem to have taught us very different lessons,'' he said harshly.

She nodded. ''Yes. I've learned to value love more highly than anything else in life. You've learned to fear it so much that you never want to find it. We've reached the same point by opposite paths.''

''Are we at the same point?'' he asked, almost holding his breath for the answer.

She looked at him. ''We're both alone. The difference is that you prefer it that way.''

He grew pale, as though her words were a lance that had probed a painful place in his heart. No one in his life had seen past his barriers so clearly—no one except Kaspar. ''It remains to be seen which of us is the wiser,'' he said, with slightly forced irony. ''I doubt if we shall ever convince each other.''

''I have to believe that I can convince you,'' she said. ''For Anna and Kaspar, everything depends on it.''

With a sense of shock, he remembered again that whatever she said or did was directed toward one end. He poured her some wine and spoke lightly, ''Aren't you forgetting your own grandfather? Perhaps he was really the 'great love' of her life.''

"Oh, no, it had nothing to do with him. He was a kind man in his way, but very solid and unemotional. That may have been why she married him. I think she wanted children, to give her life some meaning, and she picked a man who wouldn't notice that he didn't have all of her. She was right about him, too. He always said it was 'worth everything to have a wife who could make a good stew.' "

Despite himself, Conrad smiled faintly. "How did they meet?"

"He was on a walking holiday through Germany, and he passed through Hamburg, where she was working. He said he was going down as far as Munich and when he came back he was 'thinking of' proposing to her."

"But you don't think he was smitten with love at first sight?" Conrad asked, with a touch of irony.

Laurel shrugged. "He was twenty years older than her and he'd always lived with his mother, who'd just died. He was feeling lost and in need of looking after. Gran made him a pie. He used to grow lyrical about that pie years afterward."

"When did they marry?" Conrad asked suddenly.

"Nineteen thirty-four."

"Three years after she left my grandfather." Conrad sighed and shook his head. "It makes no sense."

"My mother was their only child," Laurel continued. "My parents died when I was very young, and after that I lived with my grandparents. But it was Anna who brought me up. Grandpa had his beer and his racing pigeons, and that was all he really wanted."

Every word she said made Conrad more uneasy. His vision of Anna Morgan had always been of an icy goddess, dancing through life, breaking hearts casually and then moving on. Laurel's picture of a woman settling for a humdrum marriage to man whose highest praise was reserved for her cooking didn't fit. It was impossible to hate that sad woman, a fact that disconcerted him more than anything else. "It certainly doesn't sound like a love match," he agreed.

"That's why I soon realized there must have been someone else. Grandpa died when I was fourteen, and I felt free to ask her if there was a man she'd loved before she'd met my grandfather. I'll never forget the light that came into her eyes as she said, 'Before, and now, and always.' She didn't tell me his name, just that they'd loved each other very much, and that they'd been together for a short time. But she said when love was as deep as theirs, an hour could be made to last a lifetime."

Laurel's eyes shone as she said this, and his hand tightened on his glass. The words were uncannily reminiscent of Kaspar's "one moment of glory... to last forever," but Conrad was a practical man, happiest with certainties, and the echo increased his inner turmoil. Then he looked at Laurel, her eyes alight with the reflected flames of the candles, and he knew that Anna had once shared this thought with her lover, and that as she did so, she had looked just like this.

"Why were you given that name?" he asked abruptly. "It has to be more than coincidence."

She smiled. "It was Gran's doing. She practically ordered my poor parents to call me Laurel, and they gave in. She was a very strong woman, but then, she'd have to be, wouldn't she, to love your grandfather as much as she did and give him up. It must have taken great strength."

"You forget, I haven't agreed that she loved him. I never saw her. I only saw the results of her destruction."

"But *I* saw her, and I know. I know that after all those years and so many miles apart, they're still linked by an unbreakable bond. How else could he have sensed her death?"

Conrad stared at her. "What do you mean?"

"He collapsed on the very same day she died. In his heart he knew what had happened."

He took a deep breath, trying to steady himself. "That is nothing but a coincidence, as you must very well know."

"I don't believe in that kind of coincidence," she said passionately. "I know they're still part of each other. The last thing she did in her life was to reach out to him. Just before she died, she told me he was the man she'd always loved, and made me promise to give him her final message. That's why I'm here, why I'm fighting so hard to make you let me see him. Oh Conrad, please, you *must* believe me. It's so terribly important to them."

He didn't answer directly. After a while he said, "What is this message? I must know. I won't have him upset."

"The packet is sealed. I don't know what's inside."

"Then open it and show me."

"But I can't do that! Can't you see why I can't?" she cried. "It's between them. Anna would never hurt him—"

"Indeed," he said ironically.

"Yes, you think I'm crazy for saying that, don't you? But it wasn't lack of love that drove her away. I *know* that." Laurel's voice grew desperate. She would

never have a better chance than this, and she must not
fail. She was pleading not just for the present, but for
the past, for two young lovers whose bright dawn had
been cruelly turned into night. The power to restore
that brightness had been placed in her hands. But she
could only use it by finding a way to the heart of this
stubborn, difficult man, and touching it with her own
love for him. "She sent me here to heal that old
wound," she said. "Once I've seen him, he can be
happy again. You *must* let it happen. You must trust
her love."

"How can I trust something I don't believe in?"
Conrad demanded. "*You* say she loved him, and
he—"

He broke off as he saw what he was revealing, but
Laurel was too quick for him. "He says so too, doesn't
he?" she urged.

"His mind is failing. He believes what he wants to.
He's dying. Leave him in peace."

"But that's what he's waiting for. He'll only find
peace when he's reassured of her love."

"Laurel, be reasonable. She stayed with him only
briefly, when it's set against the years he was without
her. I can't believe that moment in time can still be all
that counts for him."

"But if love is real, time doesn't mean anything.
They always understood that."

"And so do you, that's what you mean to say, isn't
it?" he demanded. "The only one who's too stupid to
understand is me, apparently. But why should I accept
your word for it? Who made you their ambassador?"

"They did," she responded at once. "Anna, who
sent me here, and Kaspar, who's waiting for me. You

must let me go to him, Conrad, not because I want it—but because *they* want it.''

Conrad was seized by alarm. He was so close to yielding, and it would be so easy to let her passionate fervor sweep him away. Her eyes were shining with entreaty, and something else that almost overwhelmed him. He was being pulled toward the shoals and if he didn't make one last desperate effort, he would be lost. "Love destroys as well as creates," he said harshly. "It's done too much damage to my family, and I won't allow it to do any more. *Do you understand that?*''

Without giving her a chance to answer he rose abruptly, thrust some money in the waiter's hand, and strode out, leaving her looking after him in dismay. The street was dark and still, and he leaned against the wall, trying to regain his equilibrium. He felt ashamed of his outburst, but he'd had to escape her subtle spell while there was still time.

Then, he wondered why he still tried to delude himself. There was no time. There never had been.

After a moment, she emerged. "I'm sorry," he said somberly. "I didn't mean to shout at you. I like to think of myself as a calm, rational person, but—not with you, not about this."

"I know. It matters too much."

She took the arm that he offered, and they walked together in silence for a few minutes before he felt her wince and stop. "What is it?''

"I don't walk very well yet."

He groaned. "Damn my thoughtlessness! I actually forgot about that. You left your cane in the square, didn't you?" He took the black velvet cloak that she'd snatched up in her rush to join him outside and put it around her shoulders, pulling her hair free and letting it run sensuously through his fingers. "Do you think *he* did this?" he asked, a brooding look on his face.

"Yes," she breathed.

"And this?" He drew her close and tightened his arms around her. Laurel raised her face for the kiss she'd been waiting for yearningly since the last time, and a sigh escaped her as she felt the touch of his lips on hers at last.

"Yes..." she murmured. "Yes...yes..." not knowing any longer whether she meant the other pair of lovers, or herself and the man who possessed her heart so completely.

"Yes," Conrad echoed, "he did this because he couldn't help himself. The spell is too strong. Set me free, Lorelei."

"I can't," she murmured, dazed at the touch of his lips moving magically over hers. "The spell is too strong for me, too."

She slipped an arm around his neck, drawing his head further down so that she could kiss him fervently. She was trying to weave the spell even more powerfully, fearful that he would manage to break free from its toils. But his answering passion told her he was no longer struggling. Whatever might happen between them in the future, he was hers tonight, as she was his forever.

They drew apart, trembling with the force of their desire, and he looked down at her. "I promised myself that I wouldn't yield to you again," he said. "I meant to be strong, to tell you to leave my home tomorrow, but I can't...*I can't...*"

Before she could speak, he bent and lifted her in a movement that echoed their first meeting. Only now it was different. Now she could hear his heart beating against her own and his breath coming raggedly as their bodies communicated heat. As he began to walk along the street, Laurel put her arms around his neck and rested her head against his shoulder. "Where are we going?" she whispered.

"I don't know. We ought to go home."

"I suppose we should," she agreed reluctantly.

"Do you want to?"

"No."

"Nor I." Even the will to resist was slipping away from him now. She was in his arms, and even if his life had depended on it, he knew he couldn't give up that feeling of sweetness. As he walked, he kissed her, and his feet headed for the river as if of their own accord. Within sight of the water, he set her down.

Laurel saw that the whole town seemed to have congregated on the bank, looking eagerly up to the sky, where a host of sparkling lights glowed against the darkness. Fireworks were being set off from three launches in the middle of the river, and around them bobbed a multitude of little boats.

Conrad looked around until he caught the eye of a man in the crowd. The man made a gesture to show that he understood, and began to walk on ahead. "His name is Ulrich," Conrad explained as they followed. "Sometimes I hire his boat."

Ulrich led them to the water's edge and down the steps to where his little cabin cruiser was moored. Conrad helped Laurel into the cabin and closed the doors, shutting out the rest of the world, enclosing them in silence. As the boat began to chug gently away from the shore, he took her in his arms again.

Laurel responded with heartfelt fervor, giving herself up to his kiss. They were free now of the problems and antagonism that filled their everyday encounters. They were only a man and a woman bound by mutual passion and growing love.

He uttered her name over and over as he kissed her, but whether he said "Laurel," or "Lorelei," she couldn't tell. And then his tongue was in her mouth, exploring her slowly, leaving trails of fire wherever it touched. She gave a long sigh of pleasure and answered him with sensuous movements and caresses. His strong, yet gentle touch delighted her, and her whole being seemed to flower in his arms.

At last she felt him draw away a little, and slowly, as if awakening from a long, sweet dream, she opened her eyes. She was lying back against the cushions, in Conrad's arms. In the light from the windows, she could just make out his features as he gazed down at her. Suddenly, she heard a faint whirring. The darkness behind him seemed to part, revealing stars and a thousand glittering lights. "Ulrich has made the roof slide back," Conrad explained, "so that you can see the fireworks."

He dropped his head and began to run his lips gently along the line of her jaw. Dazed, she watched the exploding colors of the rockets far above her head, and they mingled with the explosions of sensation wherever his lips touched her. Forks of light danced through her as he moved down the length of her neck to where his tongue could flicker against the hollow of her throat, and she drew in a long, shuddering breath. She loved him so much.

He began to move his hands over her body, touching her through the flimsy material of her dress. She ached to feel him against her skin, and when he pulled the dress down from her shoulders so that he could lay his cheek against one exposed breast, she shuddered with delight. "Never leave me," he whispered.

She wasn't sure she'd heard him correctly, but he said the words again. "Stay.... Don't go away... Stay forever."

Conrad was barely conscious of speaking. The words seemed to have been drawn by some irresistible force from a well of passionate feeling inside him, so deeply buried that he hadn't known it was there. But it had always been there, awaiting the woman who could make it overflow. Now it was governing his every word and action, making him say incredible things and admit to desires he'd sought vainly to deny. It urged him now to explore the heart of her mystery, for only there could he find the secret that would make sense of his life. The words, "I need you," broke from him. "Don't ever leave me."

He sensed, rather than heard, the vibration in her soft flesh as she answered. He looked up and saw her lips move in what might have been a promise or a denial. But the answer was revealed in her shining eyes— a joyous affirmation that she, too, was caught up in the emotions and sensations that were rocking his being.

He smiled, feeling an unequivocal happiness he'd never known before, and feasted his eyes on her. The fireworks caused the light to come and go, dancing over her in many colors, giving her an other-worldly look that once would have made him wary. Now he could only stare, entranced, and when she raised a hand to touch his cheek with her fingertips, he trembled and seized it, burying his face in her palm, his lips burning her skin. He felt her pulse leap in response and continued his exploration, letting his lips drift along her inner arm, until her loveliness overwhelmed him. He groaned, laying his head against her breasts and feeling her arms enfold him. "Hold me," he whispered against her heart.

A sense of unutterable peace and freedom pervaded him. The troubles that had seemed important before were retreating, even as the shore retreated from the boat. The only reality was here, in her arms, as the two of them let the river carry them into infinity. Fireworks whizzed and crackled, and the gorge caught the sounds and replayed them with endless hollow echoes. High above them, the rock was dimly outlined in the moonlight, serene and aloof amid the enchanted sounds that cascaded in an endless shower.

He felt the slight rocking of the boat that meant Ulrich had traveled as far downstream as he dared and was halting, ready to retrace his journey. As they turned, the banks slid past and Laurel pointed through the window. Conrad followed her gesture and saw Feldstein Castle come into view. It had been floodlit for the carnival, and now its towers and turrets gleamed against the darkness. The whole building seemed to float serenely above the trees that covered the slope below.

"Did you ever see anything so magical?" Laurel breathed.

She wondered if the down-to-earth Conrad would reject the notion of magic, but he seemed transfixed by what he saw. "No," he said at last. "I hadn't realized it was so lovely."

A pang of dread went through him as he thought of the danger that threatened his beloved home. Tomorrow he must set out for Munich to seek the finances that would put chains on Feldstein Castle. He should have spent tonight working on figures, preparing himself for the battle, instead of listening to the siren's song. Dread was replaced by guilt at the way the Lorelei had made him forget everything but herself. He rubbed a hand over his eyes as though trying to force himself awake. "I think we should go back," he said unsteadily.

Laurel heard the changed note in his voice, and followed his thoughts accurately. If only, she thought, she could admit that she knew what troubled him. But she didn't know how he'd take it, and it was too great a risk.

At a signal from Conrad, Ulrich headed for the shore. They docked a short walk from the town square, and made their way through streets that were now almost empty, except for one or two stragglers trailing home in fancy dress. The carnival was over. In the square, the tables and chairs had been cleared away, and only a few lamps were left to shine faintly on the cobblestones. The night was growing chilly, but it wasn't the cold air that made Laurel shiver. It was the knowledge that the magic was dying, and only the problems remained.

They found her cane neatly leaning against a wall. She'd soared to the heavens that night, but as she lifted the cane she seemed to become earthbound again.

"I have to go away tomorrow," Conrad said. "I'll be gone for about two days. When I come back..."

He hesitated. A breeze had sprung up, making her hair billow slightly to form a frame about her face. He wanted to touch her, to experience again the sweetness that had tempted him to drift on forever with her and never look back. But it was too late. The moment couldn't be recaptured.

"It's time we were going," he said heavily. "I still have a lot of work to do."

Chapter Nine

At breakfast the next morning, Conrad refused most of the food set before him and took only black coffee and rolls. His face was pale and set, and he responded to Friederich's teasing about the possible purpose of his "mysterious" journey with only a brief smile. Laurel found herself angry with Friederich, whose youthful thoughtlessness protected him from the problems Conrad had to bear.

From time to time, Conrad raised his eyes and fixed them on Laurel. She was almost certain he was thinking the same thing as she was—if only they could have a moment alone, instead of having to behave so formally in front of the others. But no opportunity came, and at last he rose and strode out of the castle to where his car was waiting for him. Horst danced along by his side, Johanna gave him a sisterly kiss and Friederich adjured him to "behave yourself, you sly dog." Conrad gave Laurel a brief half-smile over everyone's head, before getting into the car and driving away.

Laurel's heart went with him. She thought of the picture Anna had left her, but the hundred thousand pounds it would fetch was nowhere near the amount Conrad needed. Unless a miracle happened, he would have to mortgage the castle, and she knew that would break his heart.

As she went inside, Johanna waylaid her. "I've been hoping for a chance to apologize for my behavior last night," she said. "I shouldn't have shouted at you, but I was so worried about Horst that I lost control of myself. Please forgive me."

"Of course," Laurel said warmly. "I'm just glad it all ended well."

"Except that Horst is now nagging me to have the Kaufmanns here," Johanna said with a rueful smile. "I suppose I shall have to say yes, or he'll run off himself, to find them."

"You don't really mind that they're bakers, do you?" Laurel asked.

"You find that strange? These old social distinctions often carry a lot of sense behind them. It's easy for children to be friends, but what happens whey they grow up and their different backgrounds start to show?"

"Their friendship will either be strong enough to overcome the differences, or it will fade naturally," Laurel said. "Even if it fades, Horst will be better off for having known them. But I don't think that will happen. Horst has a warm heart. I think he'll keep his friends for life."

She managed to change the subject, not wanting to sour the atmosphere with views that her hostess obviously considered revolutionary, and Johanna's manner reverted to its normal reserved amiability.

On the second day of Conrad's absence they had lunch together, with Horst. When the little boy had bounced off to play in the garden, Johanna observed, "You're very silent."

"I'm sorry, I didn't mean to be rude," Laurel said hastily. "It's just that I've got a lot on my mind."

Johanna poured her some more coffee. "Why don't you tell me what's troubling you?"

"It's the baron. I originally came here to deliver something to him. I didn't know he was seriously ill. I thought it would be easy. But Conrad is determined to stop me from seeing him."

"So I gather. But can it matter to the baron now, anyway? Everything is in Conrad's hands. Surely you can deliver whatever it is to him?"

"No, it's very personal." Laurel hesitated. But Johanna was a woman and would surely understand about love. "It's a message from my grandmother," she said at last. "He loved her once. But to Conrad, that's another reason for keeping me out. My injured ankle was a godsend, because it forced him to let me into the castle."

"But surely your ankle is much better now?"

"Yes, it is, but I won't go without doing what I came to do."

Johanna was toying with the stem of her glass, and seemed determined to avoid Laurel's eyes as she asked, "So this is why you continue to stay here?"

"It's become a battle of wills between Conrad and me, and he wins every time. I hoped I could teach him to trust me, but . . ." Laurel shrugged.

Johanna nodded. "Conrad is very strict about protecting his family. That's good, but sometimes he goes
a little too far. Why shouldn't you see the baron if it's
important?"

"It's desperately important," Laurel said passionately. "But Helga's in charge of the sickroom, and both
she and Brigitta have orders not to let me in."

"They are employees and naturally do what they're
told," Johanna said. She sat lost in thought for a few
moments. Then she looked directly at Laurel and
added, with meaning, "But *I'm* not an employee."

Laurel stared at her with an expression of incredulous hope. "Johanna, do you really mean that you'd
help me?" she said breathlessly.

"Why not? They can't refuse *me*."

"Could we do it now?"

Johanna looked at her watch. "Now would be a
good time. Brigitta will be on duty."

"I have to fetch something first."

"Meet me in the library at the foot of the tower."

Laurel went to her room and took out Anna's package. Her heart was beating with anticipation to think
she might be nearing her goal at last. She returned to
the tower as quickly as she could and slipped into the
library.

"I want you to wait here while I go upstairs," Johanna said. "Keep the door ajar and watch for Brigitta to leave. When she's gone, you can come up."

"Suppose she won't go."

"She will. I'll send her on an errand. She won't
bother to lock the outer door with me there." Johanna hurried away.

Laurel waited, grinding her nails into her palm with
dread that something might go wrong now, when she

was so close. But after a few minutes, she saw Brigitta emerge and walk away into the main body of the house. When she was out of sight, Laurel slipped into the tower and made her way to the door at the foot of the stairs. It was open for once, and she began to climb the winding staircase. It was difficult with her leg still in plaster, and by the time she reached the top she was weary and gasping.

"Thank goodness you're here," Johanna said. "Brigitta could be back at any time. Hurry."

The massive oak door to the baron's room seemed to bar her way solidly, but when Laurel tried the handle, it opened easily. She went in softly and stood a moment, taking in the old-fashioned room with its dark, heavy furniture, and the carved oak four-poster bed in the center. She made her way to the bed as quietly as she could, clutching the precious package to her breast.

An old man lay back against the pillows, his eyes closed in sleep. His lined face was very thin, and what little hair he had was white, but Laurel could see in him traces of the handsome young giant Anna had loved long ago. She crept closer and sank onto a chair beside the bed, scarcely daring to breathe.

She wished he would awaken. She had so little time. She looked around in agitation, and that was when her eyes fell on the picture of the Lorelei at the foot of the bed. She rose and went to stand in front of it, full of excitement as she realized that the baron must have ordered it brought here, and what that signified.

"Anna...." The sound was so soft that she hardly heard it, but then it was repeated. "Anna...." It was a long, sighing whisper from the depths of a man's heart.

Laurel turned to Kaspar, and saw that he was awake. He seemed to be looking over her shoulder, his eyes fixed, with almost painful eagerness, on the picture behind her. But then Laurel moved quickly around the bed to come close to him, and his eyes followed her. *"Anna...."* he breathed with incredulous hope, his hand outstretched to her.

Suddenly she realized that her striking resemblance to her grandmother had tricked him. He remembered Anna as a young woman, and Laurel seemed like his beloved come back. She leaned close, smiling to reassure him, and reached out a gentle hand, meaning to lay it over his. But she was halted by the sound of angry voices in the next room, then a sharp intake of breath just behind her. She whirled and saw Helga glaring at her. "Fräulein, I must ask you to leave here immediately," she said firmly.

"Helga, please go away—just for a moment," Laurel pleaded.

Helga's face set in grim lines. "I will not go until you have left this room.

Laurel was in despair. She'd come so close to succeeding in her mission, but the things she had to say to Kaspar couldn't be spoken in Helga's fire-breathing presence. She gave a last desperate glance at the old man, who had closed his eyes again, and turned to the door.

And then she stopped, electrified.

Right next to the door was something so extraordinary that she could hardly believe her eyes. She took a quick step forward and stood, riveted, studying the object that suddenly, unbelievably, revived all her hope. If what she was seeing was true, it was a miracle....

"Fräulein!" Helga snapped angrily.

"All right, I'm going." Laurel limped hastily out the door.

Johanna was waiting for her in the anteroom. "I couldn't override Helga," she said apologetically. "She takes her orders from Conrad. Did you do what you wanted?"

"No, but it doesn't matter," Laurel told her, the words almost falling over each other in her excitement. "Something wonderful has happened. I can't explain, but if I'm right, it could be the answer to all Conrad's prayers—and mine."

"Indeed?" Johanna's voice was suddenly chilly, but Laurel was too absorbed in her whirling thoughts to notice. She began to limp hurriedly down the winding staircase, too exhilarated to be careful and almost falling in her urgency.

"I have to go home right now," she said when they reached the bottom. "But I'll be back as soon as I can."

"You're leaving?" Johanna queried.

"Only for a day—perhaps two." She was making her way to her room, with Johanna at her heels. Once there, she pulled out a small bag and began throwing in her overnight things.

"How will you travel?" Johanna asked.

"Flying is quickest."

"I'll call the airport."

As soon as Johanna had gone, Laurel sat down and tried to write a letter to Conrad, but it was hard to find the right words.

You will hear that I got into your grandfather's room. Don't blame me too much. I had to do it,

*and now I know I did the right thing in coming
here. Something important has happened. I'll be
back in a couple of days at the most. Remember
the other night. For me, nothing has changed.
Trust me.*

It didn't satisfy her, but it was the best she could do
in a rush. She folded the letter and sealed it.

After a few minutes Johanna returned. "There's a
plane for London from Frankfurt Airport in two
hours," she said. "I've booked you on it, and ordered
a taxi. You'll have to hurry to get there in time."

"Thank you. Would you give this to Conrad?"
Laurel put the letter into Johanna's hand.

"Certainly. But can't you tell me why you're rushing off? Or is it something only Conrad must know?"

"I haven't even told him," Laurel said. "It would be
too terrible if I'm wrong. I'll explain it all when I return."

"But perhaps you won't return," Johanna said in a
strange voice.

"Yes, I will. Nothing is more certain than that. I
must go now."

The taxi was already waiting for her. As it pulled
away, she looked out of the window and saw Horst
standing at an upstairs window staring at her incredulously. She waved, hoping he could see her. But if not,
she reasoned, Johanna would explain that she hadn't
gone for long.

Her eager thoughts ran ahead to England, but her
heart had been left behind with the man she loved.
When she returned, it would either be in defeat—or
with a triumphant solution to Conrad's problems.

* * *

Conrad emerged into the evening light exhausted and with a headache. He'd spent the day negotiating the huge loan he needed, on the security of the castle. His local bank had taken fright at the request and referred him to their head office in Munich. The gray men at the head office had cautiously agreed to a loan, but for only half the figure he needed. He'd been forced to apply to an institution that specialized in high risk loans. It was newly established, and he sensed an unscrupulous aura about it. Only sheer desperation had driven him through the doors.

The directors had received him with a hint of overfriendliness that suggested they'd been tipped off. He was sure of it when they produced figures that had been prepared in advance and offered him all he wanted at an extortionate rate of interest. What scared him most was that two of the directors had massive interests in a leisure park company. He knew without asking that if he fell behind on the payments, there would be no grace period. They would fall on Feldstein Castle with delight, and within a year it would have become a "Lorelei Theme Center". The prospect was appalling, unthinkable, and yet—he had no choice.

He'd refused to sign anything, but the papers were locked in his briefcase, and he knew he was only postponing the inevitable. Now he faced a drive of over seven hundred kilometers. Common sense told him he should stay in Munich tonight and start in the morning. But the ache to get home was too intense. At a small restaurant, he had a light snack of sausage with sweet-and-sour red cabbage and coffee, then headed for his car.

It was a sleek, powerful vehicle, the one touch of flamboyance he allowed himself, and despite the gathering darkness, it ate up the miles to Stuttgart. There, he stopped for some fresh air and more coffee, but weariness was beginning to claim him.

As he started on his journey again, rain hit the windscreen. He drove carefully, trying not to become hypnotized by the windshield wipers, but their deadening rhythm seemed to emphasize the weight dragging on his heart. His home was under threat, and to get it free again was going to be a task so enormous that his courage almost failed him.

Worst of all, there was no one he could tell. The habit of protecting the family was ingrained in him, and he'd always carried the burden lightly. But now he felt terrifyingly alone. Friederich was well-meaning but irresponsible, Johanna wouldn't understand, and his grandfather must not be disturbed in his last days.

The thought of his grandfather opened a door in his mind, and Laurel slipped through, bringing a stream of memories. He recalled talking with her, telling her about his dead brother and seeing the warmth and understanding in her eyes. He saw Horst giving him an impulsive hug because he was thrilled to be in the procession—*her* doing. And suddenly, in a searing moment, he realized whom he wanted to talk to. Everything became clear, and he wondered how he could ever have been such a fool.

Another memory was there: the night of the carnival, Horst's disappearance, Laurel taking him in her arms, calming his nightmares, bringing him peace—the moment when mystery and desire had been refined into pure love. So easy to see now.

How close he'd come to happiness, and how clumsily he'd nearly thrown it away! He'd denied his love, fearing it, when what he should have feared was life without her. But he'd seen the truth in time, and the truth was that he loved her with his whole being.

Suddenly, he understood why Kaspar had been haunted all his life by one woman, and nothing had ever consoled him for his loss. With the discovery, the dreadful weight on Conrad's heart seemed to lift, leaving him with a sensation of freedom. It was illogical to feel like this when his problems were as bad as ever, but he was beyond logic. One thought occupied his mind: he'd learned the secret of life.

His inner vision was so intense that he almost seemed to see her before him, retreating into the darkness of the endless road, beckoning him home where he would find joy and peace in her arms. Instinctively he put his foot down on the accelerator, but immediately he felt the car swing out of control as it began to hydroplane. He fought madly with the wheel, trying to keep away from the rock that reared up beside the road. For a dreadful moment, he was sure he was going to smash into it head-on, but he managed to swerve at the last moment. He heard a grinding crunch as the side of the car scraped the rock, and then he came to a halt so sharply that his head hit the window.

He sat dazed for a moment, his heart pounding as he realized how close he'd come to death. As he got out to inspect the damage, the cold rain lashed him, and he could already see the flashing light of a police vehicle heading in his direction.

The car drew up beside him and a policeman got out. After questioning Conrad and satisfying himself that he was completely sober, he studied the car carefully. "That's a nasty mess," he observed.

"It's only bodywork down one side," Conrad said impatiently. "I can still drive it."

"You're lucky the road was empty. You know you're mad to be driving in this weather at night, don't you? What's the urgency?"

"I wanted to get home," Conrad said shortly.

The officer looked at the address Conrad had given him. "That's another two hundred kilometers," he grunted. "I can't let you do that. You're a menace."

"But I've got to get there," Conrad almost shouted.

"Whatever is it can't be important enough to risk your neck for."

Conrad couldn't have begun to explain the feelings coursing through him to this stolid policeman. He only knew that he *had* to get back to Laurel, the only person in the world who could give his spirit the balm it needed. "It's urgent family business," he said at last.

"Sorry, it's out of the question. I'd better book you to keep you safe."

Suddenly, Conrad was frantic. Fear was growing within him, as though the world would end if he couldn't reach her tonight. "Look," he said urgently, "it's only another ten kilometers to Heidelberg. I can hire a taxi for the rest of the way."

"At this hour? Suppose you can't?"

"Then I'll book into a hotel. But I'll find a taxi. I'll *make* someone take me."

"All right. I'll follow you into town just to be on the safe side."

The car was barely usable. Conrad limped into Heidelberg and found a taxi firm that was about to close for the night. For the generous fee he offered, the boss produced a driver and promised to look after his damaged car.

In half an hour he was on the road again. As he leaned back, he realized that his head was aching from the thump it had received, and he was dead tired. He wanted to sleep, but somehow he could only hover on the verge while images came and went distractedly in his brain.

At last he fell into an uncomfortable doze in which he was aware of Laurel, not close as he wanted her to be, but far away, seated up high on a rock, luring him on. He was on a road, driving fast to get to her, driving dangerously so that he skidded and nearly ended his life by smashing against rocks. Then suddenly, the rocks were beneath him and the road had turned to water, sucking him under. He shuddered and awoke with a start.

"Better stop at the next service station," he said to the driver. "We could both use some coffee."

The coffee made him feel better. He carried it outside and stood breathing the cold night air until he was fully awake. He could smile now at the fantasy that had plagued his dreams. Perhaps he'd tell her and they could share the secret. There were so many other things, too, that he wanted to tell her, but they'd take a lifetime. A surge of happiness and release swept through him and he laughed out loud.

"Are you all right?" the driver asked him nervously.

"I am now," he said, in a voice that was full of joy. "Everything's very much all right."

It was four in the morning when he arrived home. The castle was in darkness, except for a light in the baron's tower. Mastering an impulse to awaken Laurel and tell her everything that was in his heart, he made his way directly to his grandfather's room.

He found Helga emerging. "How is he?" Conrad asked in a low voice.

"Still holding his own," Helga informed him. "Though I have to inform you that, despite my efforts, the English Fräulein managed to get into his room."

Once the news would have enraged him, but now Conrad only smiled and said, "I might have known she would manage it. I should never have kept her out."

Helga's stare was full of frosty disapproval. "I obeyed the instructions I was given, and I would like to observe that Fräulein Blake would never have succeeded in getting in if it was not for the assistance of Frau von Feldstein."

"Johanna let her in?" Conrad asked. "I wonder why. I think I'd better—"

He was checked by the sudden opening of the door. A moment later, Horst appeared in his pajamas, and flew at him, crying, "Uncle... Uncle... She's gone away... The Lorelei's gone away...."

Clutching the small, shaking body to him, Conrad tried to ignore a stab of dread. It was nonsense. He'd misheard. "What do you mean?" he demanded, pushing Horst slightly away so that he could see his face. "Try to stop crying and tell me what's happened."

"The Lorelei's gone away and she's never coming back," Horst sobbed. "She didn't even say goodbye to me, and she's gone, forever and ever." Johanna hurried in. Conrad was shocked at the sight of her. She seemed to have aged in three days. Her face was drawn and she looked ill. "What is Horst saying?" he demanded.

Johanna pulled herself up short and her hands moved nervously to draw the edges of her robe together. When she spoke, it was with effort. "Fräulein

Blake left yesterday," she said. "In a weak moment I—allowed myself to be persuaded to bring her up here. She left the castle right afterward."

"But *why*? What happened between her and grandfather?"

"I don't know. She was in there alone."

"I found her and told her to go," Helga said grimly.

"And she simply left the castle without a word of explanation?" Conrad asked. "Johanna, she must have said *something* to you."

Johanna became, if possible, paler and more ill-looking. If Conrad had any attention to spare, he might have noticed he was talking to someone who'd embarked on a difficult course from which there was no turning back. At last, Johanna said, "All she told me was that she would never return."

Conrad stared at her as the monstrous, unbelievable thing became real. "And she didn't leave me a message, or a letter?" he whispered.

Johanna swallowed. "She left you nothing."

"Obviously she got whatever she came for," Helga said grimly.

Johanna drew Horst toward her. "Don't cry, my darling. We must all try to forget her."

"She didn't say goodbye to me," Horst wept.

Suddenly, life flooded back into Conrad's frozen limbs. He ran from the room and almost hurled himself down the winding stairway. He blanked out his brain, refusing to let himself think until there was no choice but to face the reality. Emerging from the tower, he sprinted along the long corridors to Laurel's room. He flung open the door, switched the light on and stood there, breathing hard.

Her small personal possessions were gone from the dressing table, and the room had a lifeless atmosphere that told him the worst had happened. Madly he pulled open the wardrobe doors, but there was nothing inside. Her two suitcases were gone. She had cleaned out every single item, however tiny, and departed, leaving not a trace of herself behind. But for the burning memories that tortured him, he might almost have imagined that she'd ever inhabited this room.

He returned to the tower, moving slowly this time, like a man to whom all destinations were equally dreary. When he reached his grandfather's room, Johanna and Horst had gone. He entered and found the room almost in darkness, except for one small light by the bed. Kaspar's eyes were closed, but they opened at once and Conrad could see that they held a new glitter.

The old man seized his hand anxiously and pointed to the picture at the foot of the bed. *"She..."* he said hoarsely.

"I know, I know," Conrad tried to soothe him, barely taking in the words.

"She..." Kaspar repeated. "She came...to me..."

"No, Grandfather, it was someone else."

"She came...as I told you she would. I saw her."

It was useless to argue. Conrad sighed. "Very well, she came," he said.

"She was here...close to me...and smiling, as she used to."

"Did she give you something?" Conrad asked, remembering the package Laurel had always insisted she must deliver.

"No," Kaspar sighed. "She put out her hand to touch me. I was nearly in her arms, and then—then she vanished, just as she always vanished in my dreams."

"It was just another dream," Conrad said, trying to comfort the old man. "There was no one here."

"Yes... she was here, I saw her. But she went away... just like before."

"She deserted you. She has deserted both of us," Conrad said bitterly. "We've both been living in a dream, Grandfather, a beautiful, foolish dream, invented by a cruel woman for her own means."

"No... if she had been cruel, I couldn't have loved her. There was the simple proof in my heart all the time, if I'd had the wisdom to see it."

Conrad gave a harsh laugh. "I don't believe that. I, too, was almost deceived, but at least I came to my senses in time."

Kaspar was relapsing into confusion again. "Where is she?" he whispered weakly. "Find her...." There were tears on his cheeks as he drifted off to sleep.

A badly secured window flapped free, clattering against the outside wall. Conrad went over and leaned out into the lashing rain to take hold of it. In the darkness he couldn't see the rock, but he could hear the noises made by the storm as it echoed and re-echoed down through the gorge. Each wave of sound seemed to die away into melancholy before being renewed and flung from bank to bank, like a never ending voice raised in doleful singing.

"Damn her!" he cried out to the night and the storm. *"Damn her."*

Chapter Ten

Laurel's plane was due for departure at seven in the evening, but she arrived to find the air traffic controllers had started a slowdown. The airport looked like a refugee station, and she spent an uncomfortable night in the departure lounge, while the airline announced a string of "imminent departures", all of which turned out to be false. She finally got away the next morning, which was a Saturday, and landed in London just after noon.

She took a taxi to her apartment, stopping on the way for some groceries. It was a miserable day, with gray skies and a light rain falling. When she reached her home, the air was cold and the shabby little rooms might have looked cheerless but for the glow of hope that lit up everything around her.

When she'd warmed herself, she settled down by the phone and dialed. As she listened to the ringing, she crossed her fingers. "Mr. Taunton?" she said at last, eagerly. "This is Laurel Blake. I'm sorry to trouble you at home, but it's urgent."

"Laurel Blake?" the elderly man sounded as though he were trying to place her.

"I brought a picture to show you a few weeks ago. You said it was worth about a hundred thousand pounds on its own, but a great deal more if I had the other one of the pair. You gave me your home number to call if ever I—"

"Good grief!" he interrupted her excitedly. "Yes, I remember now. You don't mean you've actually got the other picture?"

"I know where it is. I saw it hanging on the wall of a castle in Germany. You did say the artist was German, didn't you?"

"Albrecht Steegan, eighteenth century painter, born in Munich," Mr. Taunton said. "I remember being surprised to see one of his works in England. It was a small oil painting of the Rhine gorge at sunset, wasn't it?"

"That's right. And you told me its companion would be the same view at dawn. That's what I saw. I'm sure it is."

"And it's still over there? Most interesting. I wonder how they came to be separated."

"I think I know how that happened. I've come back to get my picture out of the bank. I should have arrived last night, but the plane was late and when I got here the banks had closed. Now I'll have to wait until Monday."

"Until Tuesday, I'm afraid. Monday's a public holiday. The banks won't be open."

"Oh, heavens!" she exclaimed in dismay. "I've been away so long, I've lost track of English holidays. I called because you said your firm had branches all over Europe."

"Certainly. I can put you in touch with our Munich office, and they'll send an expert to verify the other picture. Do I understand that you don't actually own the other one? That could be a problem."

A radiant smile illuminated her face. "I don't think it will be," she said joyfully. "Goodbye. I'll be in touch."

She put down the phone and wandered about restlessly. It was maddening to have this sudden extra delay when she longed to confirm the good news and tell Conrad. She thought of his face, how it would look when the shadows lifted from it, and she was swept with longing for him. He seemed so far away and the world was so desolate without him.

She made herself a meal, but it was an effort to eat. Then, without warning, the previous night's lack of sleep caught up with her, and she just managed to reach the bed before her eyes closed.

She slept without stirring until the next morning and awoke to find herself fully clothed. Eagerly, she called the castle. Perhaps Conrad had returned and she could at least talk to him. After three days apart, the need to hear his voice was an ache inside her. Johanna answered the phone. "Has your trip proved successful?" she asked politely.

"It's too soon to say, but I'm hopeful. Johanna, is Conrad back yet?"

It seemed to Laurel that Johanna hesitated a fraction of a second before saying, "No."

"He hasn't called to say when he expects to come home?"

"I'm afraid not. You must realize that he's very busy."

"Yes, of course," Laurel said, feeling a little dashed. Then she remembered something. "I'm sorry I had to hurry off without saying goodbye to Horst. I saw him looking out of the window. Did you tell him I'll be coming back?"

"Don't worry, I explained everything to Horst."

"Can I have a word with him?"

"I'm afraid not. He's away for the weekend, visiting with my parents."

"Oh. He didn't tell me he was going away."

Johanna gave an odd, artificial laugh. "But why should he tell you? In any case, my parents invited him very suddenly. I must go now. Goodbye." She hung up before Laurel could answer.

Laurel replaced the receiver, feeling slightly puzzled. There was a strange frostiness in Johanna's manner, and something else that might almost have been desperation. Then she shrugged and told herself she was imagining things. Some people's voices were distorted by the telephone.

Somehow she got through the rest of Sunday, reading mail that had accumulated, considering work offers, writing letters. But her heart wasn't in any of it, and Conrad's face seemed to get between her and whatever she was doing. When she slept, she found she was in his arms again, his lips burning hers. But then she'd awake and find herself alone, and the yearning for him was almost intolerable.

She finally fell into a light doze in the early hours of Monday, and was awakened by the sound of her front doorbell. Shrugging into a robe, she opened the door and found a man standing outside. "Telegram," he said cheerfully. "Sign here please."

Laurel signed and closed the door, wondering who could be sending her a telegram. Then she saw that it had been sent from Hargen, and swiftly tore it open. As she read the contents, she grew very still.

DO NOT TRY TO RETURN STOP YOU WILL NOT BE AL-
LOWED IN STOP CONRAD VON FELDSTEIN

She sat down, her heart thumping, and tried to understand what she read. How could Conrad have turned against her? The night of the carnival, he'd come close to saying he loved her, and in her heart she'd been sure that he did. When he left, he'd looked at her in such a way that her heart had turned over, and she'd known that when he returned it would be to her. Now the telegram in her hand seemed to make a mockery of all her certainty.

While she stared at it, the doorbell sounded again. Eagerly, she jumped up and ran to answer it. It would be another telegram, saying that the first had been a mistake.

But outside stood a man with a huge box at his feet. "Special delivery from Germany," he said. "A place called..." he squinted. "Hargen. Is that right? D'you know anyone in Hargen?"

"Yes," she said in a bleak voice. "I know someone there."

She signed mechanically and pulled the box inside, almost shaking with dread. It was just large enough to hold all the baggage she'd left behind, but surely that was impossible. Surely...

She tore it open and drew in a sharp breath as she saw her large suitcase and all the clothes she'd left behind. The hideous truth lay there. Conrad had not only banished her, he'd pulled up the drawbridge behind her.

She seized the phone and called the castle. It seemed ages before she heard the number ring, but when it did, Johanna answered so quickly that she might almost have been waiting for the call. "Hello," she said curtly.

"Johanna, it's Laurel."

There was sudden silence before Johanna said, "What do you want?" in an odd, muffled voice.

"Conrad has sent me a telegram saying I mustn't come back, along with my clothes. I don't understand it."

"What is there to understand? You stayed here while you were ill. Now you're recovered. That's all."

"Yes, but—there's more to it than that. Conrad and I—I can't explain on the telephone, but I *must* speak with him," Laurel said desperately.

"He doesn't want to speak to you."

"But *why*?"

Johanna hesitated. "You mustn't ask me that. It has nothing to do with me."

"But you must know something. Did you give him my note?"

"Of course I did," Johanna said stiffly. "I'm sorry, but I can't help you. Goodbye."

"No, wait," Laurel said quickly, before Johanna could put down the phone. "There's something you haven't told me."

"I don't know what you mean."

"You sound as if you've been crying. What's happened?"

Johanna's voice rose to shrillness. "Nothing's happened. I'm not crying. How dare you! Why don't you just stay away and stop bothering us? We were all right before you came." She slammed the phone down, but not before Laurel distinctly heard a sob.

She still had one hope. It wasn't a public holiday in Germany, and soon Conrad would be at work. She spent the worst hour of her life waiting for the hands of the clock to crawl forward, then lifted the phone again, and in a few moments was through to the distillery.

"I'd like to speak to Herr von Feldstein," she said, her heart thumping.

"Your name, please?"

For a wild moment she thought of giving a false name, to be sure of getting through to him, but she abandoned the idea at once. If Conrad was hostile to her now, a deception would make him even more so. She gave her name and at once the operator said, "I'm afraid you can't speak to Herr von Feldstein."

"*Please,* it's terribly important."

"But he is not here," said the operator firmly.

"When do you expect him?"

"He won't be in today, maybe not for several days."

"Can you tell me where he's gone?" Laurel asked desperately.

"I'm afraid not. Can anyone else help you?"

"No. Thank you very much," Laurel said automatically, and laid down the phone. She longed to believe in this mysterious absence, but all her instincts told her that she'd been put off again. Conrad was there, and he'd instructed his staff not to put her through. Suddenly, she was filled with terror. This had to be a nightmare, one from which she would awaken to find everything as it should be. But the moments passed and she didn't awaken.

She thought of the picture and how she'd meant to save him. But how could she do that if she couldn't even get through to him? Nonetheless, she must pull herself together and get on with what she'd come here to do. She drank some black coffee, took a shower, and dressed. She was functioning on automatic, concentrating on practical things to avoid being too conscious of the anguish in her heart.

At the bank, she gave her deposit box number and was shown through into the vault, where she retrieved the picture. It was a small canvas, eighteen inches by twenty-four, but painted with such subtlety that the whole Rhine gorge seemed to lie before her, bathed in the glorious light of sunset, just as she remembered it. Despite her emotional turmoil, she experienced a stab of excitement. This *must* be the companion to the one she'd seen on Kaspar's wall. The view was exactly the same. Only the lighting was different.

She packed it up in some cardboard and brown paper she'd brought with her, signed a receipt, and left the bank. She hailed a cab, but as she was about to give her address she was stopped by a thought. Mr. Taunton had promised her an introduction to an expert in Munich. If she went to see him now, she could get it at once and be on her way back to Germany tomorrow. "Taunton Fine Art on Bond Street, please," she told the driver.

Ten minutes later she stepped into the discreetly luxurious establishment and approached the receptionist. "I'd like to speak to Mr. Taunton, please. It's Laurel Blake."

"I'm afraid you've just missed him. He's gone to an appointment, and won't be back today."

Laurel groaned. She should have called first. Now she would have to wait until tomorrow. She went out into the street, feeling depressed, and hailed another cab. Suddenly there was no way of escaping her own feelings. The mountain she would have to climb even to contact Conrad seemed to loom before her, enormous and threatening. The painting might be her last chance, and she clutched it closely to her.

The taxi drew up outside the shabby apartment block and she climbed out, ducking to avoid the drizzle that had started. Inside, she studied the mail boxes, clutching at the hope that there would be something from him. But her own slot was empty, and she began to trudge up the stairs to her front door. The package was starting to feel heavy and her arm ached.

Preoccupied, she didn't notice a shadow on her dimly lit landing that grew very still at her approach. She hurried into her apartment and put the picture down quickly, and then she heard the front door close behind her. A quiet voice said, "Lorelei."

Laurel froze in wild disbelief. Dreams didn't come true like this in real life. And yet . . .

She whirled and saw Conrad.

He was gazing at her with desperate intensity, a world of anguish and hope in his eyes. "Lorelei," he said again, as though his lips could barely shape the words. "Lorelei, *why did you leave me?*"

"But I—" She could hardly speak for emotion. Her gaze was fixed on Conrad's face, where she saw something she'd thought she would never see again. There was no condemnation, only passionate, heartfelt love. She took a step forward at the very same moment he moved toward her, and in the next second, they were in each other's arms.

All heartache disappeared as she felt his mouth hard on hers and his arms holding her close. There was so much she wanted to say to him, but words could never express it. Only the eloquence of her caressing hands, the subtlety of her lips returning his kiss, the trembling of her body against his, could tell him all the thousand wonderful things she wanted him to know.

"Why did you go?" he breathed as he kissed her. "Why? *Why?*" But he smothered her mouth again, before she could answer. Her heart leaped because she could feel that this kiss was different from any other he'd given her. All of his soul was in it, with none of the resistance that had been there before.

"Conrad..." she began eagerly.

"No, don't speak," he said, laying a gentle hand over her mouth. "Don't say anything until you've heard me out. I don't know why you ran away, nor what I did to make you go, but I've come to take you back. You *must* return to me or else—" He drew a shuddering breath and took her face between his hands. "Or else let me hear you say that you don't love me."

"You'll never hear me say that," she said with surprise. "Conrad, surely you know I love you?"

"I thought I did," he said, still with his eyes fixed on her face. "I was sure...but then you left without a word to me, and suddenly I couldn't be sure of anything. I hated you. Then the strangest thing happened. I don't understand it. I can only tell you how it felt.

"I stood at the window of Kaspar's room, looking out at the Lorelei rock through the darkness, and cursing you with all the bitterness in my soul. In reply I heard echoes ringing through the gorge, sounding like a lament. I recalled everything we shared that night on the boat, how lovely you were, and how completely we seemed to belong together. Perhaps I was crazy, but the melancholy singing seemed to come from the Lorelei, seemed to be reproaching my lack of faith in you.

"Suddenly, I remembered what Kaspar told me: that if only he could have found Anna, he would have challenged her to say to his face that she didn't love him. He didn't believe she could say it. I knew then what *I* had to do—find you and demand to hear *you* say it." He searched her face. "If you could have done so, there would have been nothing left for me in this life."

She answered him by drawing his hand down to hers and laying her lips on his in reassurance. She felt his arms tighten around her again, and she became oblivious to everything except the happiness of being with him. There were still a thousand questions puzzling her, but the only vital question had already been answered forever.

"Swear to come back to me," he said at last. "Swear to marry me and never leave my side again. I won't let you go until you do. I was a blind fool for so long, but tell me it isn't too late."

"Darling," she said, half laughing, half crying with the bittersweet power of her emotion, "I can't follow anything you're saying."

"Then listen carefully," he said, speaking in a low, intense voice. "I love you with all my heart and soul. I shall love you until I die, and beyond. I'm going to marry you, whatever you say. If you don't agree now, I'll keep asking until you do. If it takes ten years, I'll persuade you in the end. Is that plain enough?"

"It won't take ten years," she told him huskily. "It won't take ten seconds. Oh, darling, I don't know what's happening. I only know I love you more than anyone in the world, and I'll always belong to you. Hold me tight, as tight as you can."

He did as she asked, crushing her until she was breathless. "Why did you go?" he murmured into her hair. "Did I do something wrong?"

"But—didn't you get my note?"

"What note?"

"I wrote you that I'd be back in a couple of days. I gave it to Johanna."

He stared at her, thunderstruck. "Johanna never gave me any note. She said you'd been to see my grandfather, and then returned to England without leaving a word. Horst has been desolate because you didn't say goodbye to him."

"Only because I assumed Johanna would explain that I'd be back soon."

A hard look settled on Conrad's face. "She let me think you'd gone for good. I couldn't believe it at first, but then I saw that you'd taken all your possessions—"

"But I didn't," Laurel said urgently. "I only took a few things in an overnight bag. Someone sent the rest on after me. Look." She freed herself from him arms and showed him the packing case with her possessions that had arrived that morning. Then she held out the telegram and saw his face become even more grim as he read it. "I never sent this," he said emphatically.

"I called, but Johanna said you didn't want to speak to me."

"That wasn't true," Conrad said quickly. "I never knew you called. I thought you'd turned against me. I felt as though you'd slammed every possible door in my face. I demanded to talk to Boris, in case you'd said something to him on the way to the airport. But Johanna said you'd insisted on taking a taxi."

"I didn't. She sent for one."

"She must have been afraid you'd tell Boris you were coming back, so she eliminated the danger. When you were gone, she sent the telegram in my name and cleared out your possessions." Conrad stopped his agitated pacing and turned a baffled face on her. "But *why*? It's not like Johanna to act like this."

"I wonder if she wants to keep you unmarried for Horst's sake." Laurel said slowly. "She'd believe anything was justified if it was for him."

"Now that I think of it, she seemed very strange when I got home," Conrad mused. "She was distressed, but I thought that was because of Horst. He kept crying because he couldn't understand why you'd 'abandoned' him."

"Poor little soul," Laurel said. "What must he think of me? I'll put it right with him as soon as I get back. Perhaps that's why Johanna was so upset. The deception must have been harder than she'd realized it would be, but once she'd started, it was too late to back out."

Conrad shook his head in wonder. "So she was trying to keep us apart? How strange, then, that she should have inadvertently done so much to bring us together. It was only when I thought I'd lost you that I discovered nothing else was important. Once, I would have been too proud to go running after a woman, begging for her love. But in those days I knew nothing. When you went, I found that the only thing that mattered was finding you and hearing you say that you loved me.

"I got here as fast as I could, but you were out. I'd been waiting on that landing for nearly four hours by the time you arrived. Every time I heard footsteps, I was sure it was you. But it never was, and I died a little inside each time. People passed me on the stairs. Some of them looked at me oddly, and I began to realize how Kaspar must have felt. But I also understood why he kept on despite them. He continued searching until he dropped, and I too would never have given up while there was strength left in me." He seized her in his arms. "But now you're here, and I'll never let you go again, my darling."

She returned his kiss gloriously, but then broke away, eager to tell him her news. "Listen . . ."

"Later," he said firmly.

She let him distract her for a full minute, but then she put her hands on his chest, insisting, "It's important."

He removed her hands and began to run his lips along the line of her jaw. "What could be more important than finding each other?" he murmured.

"Can it really be *you* that said that?" she wondered aloud, trying not to be distracted by the smoldering fires he was setting off in her. "Conrad . . ."

"Yes, it was really me," he promised, "not the man I once was, but the man I am learning to be. In your arms I become reborn, and all the world is new to me. It is a world of so much beauty, and you gave it to me."

"Our world," she said blissfully.

"Yes, our world, and I never want any other."

Chapter Eleven

"Darling," she whispered at last, "please let me go. There's something I really must tell you."

With a look of foreboding, he released her. "You're not going to reveal that you're married already?"

"No, nothing like that. It's about money and business."

"The hell with both of them," he said recklessly.

"No, you must hear my good news."

"Good—?" He looked at her wryly. "Do you mean that 'grand inheritance' you were telling me about?"

"I know you've never believed in it, but you're about to find out how wrong you were. Look at this."

She unwrapped the picture, holding it up for him to see. Conrad frowned. "It reminds me of something," he said at last. "I know I've seen it before, but I'm not sure where."

"On Kaspar's wall, just by the door," she prompted him.

"That's right—no, wait, his is slightly different."

"His shows dawn, and this is sunset, but they were painted by the same artist. I inherited this from Anna, and it's worth about a hundred thousand pounds on its own. But the pair is worth a great deal more—maybe enough to solve all your financial problems."

He looked startled. "What do you know about that?"

"I overheard you talking that day at the distillery." He groaned, but she continued, "I know you need to raise money by this Friday, or mortgage the castle."

"Then you knew why I went away?"

"I guessed. I longed to say something, but I thought you'd hate me for having overheard."

"I've been wishing I could tell you. All the way back from Munich I was thinking of you, wanting you, knowing you were the only person who could comfort me. I've got the finances set up, but I don't want it—not that way." He sighed and added, "However, I haven't any choice."

"But you have. Your picture and mine together would sell for enough to cover the debts—at least, I don't know exactly how much they are, but—"

"I need at least eight hundred thousand pounds."

"We must find out quickly if we have that much. That's why I hurried back to England directly after being in Kaspar's room. I wanted to fetch my painting."

Conrad looked dazed. "I can't take this in," he said. "You say they're a pair. Then how—?"

"Kaspar must have bought them, given one to her, and kept the other."

"Darling, wait. Kaspar bought that picture in an outdoor market. His sister told me. How could it have been on sale there if it was valuable? It's a lovely pipe dream, but there must have been a mistake."

"There's no mistake," she said stubbornly.

"But it would take a miracle for it to be worth anything. And for yours to turn out to be the lost match would take another miracle."

She put her hands on his shoulders and gazed up earnestly into his face. "Well, what of that? Haven't we learned that miracles can happen?"

"I guess we have," he said slowly. "Perhaps I should trust your wisdom. I wish I knew what to believe."

The doorbell rang before she could say anything. She hurried to answer it and her heart leaped with excitement as she saw who was standing there. "Mr. Taunton," she cried. "Just the person I wanted to see."

"I thought I'd drop in with that letter of introduction I promised you," he said, looking slightly startled as she almost pulled him inside. "It gives me another chance to see the painting. Good afternoon." This last was uttered to Conrad.

"Mr. Taunton, this is Conrad von Feldstein. He has the matching picture to mine, but he doesn't think it can be valuable because it was bought in an outdoor market."

"When was that?" Mr. Taunton asked.

"About sixty years ago," Conrad informed him.

"Ah, yes. Very likely. Steegan was never much in vogue during his lifetime—too fond of accepting commissions so he could get money for drink, and then abandoning them half-done, because he was too drunk to continue. Some of his pairs were never finished. After his death, his reputation slumped even further. It only picked up about thirty years ago."

He carried Laurel's picture over to the window. "This is part of a set that was believed lost, you know. The Duke of Marksburg commissioned them as a gift for his wife, but she was less interested in art than in the artist. The duke discovered them in a compromising situation. Steegan fled and the duke imprisoned the duchess with only the pictures for company. At one time they were thought to have been buried with her. That's why they're so valuable."

"And if the other one matches..." Laurel was almost breathless with hope.

"Together, they'd be worth a million pounds."

Laurel and Conrad looked at each other, speechless. Mr. Taunton delved into his briefcase, "Here's the letter I promised you. I'll call my colleague in Munich and tell him to expect to hear from you." He looked at them benignly. "I can see that there'll be no problem about the pictures being sold as a set. I wish you every happiness, and I'll take my leave now."

Laurel made polite attempts to detain him, but he smiled and departed. As soon as he'd gone, they threw themselves into each other's arms.

"I can't believe it," Conrad said in a choking voice. "It's too much like a dream come true. And to have it happen on the day I found you—two dreams at once—"

"But dreams do come true," she told him between kisses. "You know it now."

"And I'll never doubt it again," he swore fervently. The telephone rang. "Damn!" Conrad said. "Let it wait."

"It'll be more good news," she promised him, smiling. "This is our lucky day."

But when she answered, she found herself talking to Friederich. "Conrad told me where to reach him in case of an emergency," he told her, his voice husky with emotion.

"I think something's wrong," she said, passing the receiver to Conrad. She watched as he listened to his brother, and saw his face become ashen. Without waiting for him to hang up, she began to put some things together quickly, for her heart told her what had happened.

"It's my grandfather," Conrad said, replacing the receiver. "He's had another heart attack. We have to get back as fast as possible. We may be too late..."

"We won't be," Laurel said with conviction. "He won't die before we get there. I know he won't."

"You mean, he won't die before *you* get there, don't you?" he asked, looking at her strangely.

"Perhaps I do. Try to have faith, my love."

"I must," he said slowly, "because if he dies without seeing you—and it's my fault—" He closed his eyes, as if the thought was too much to bear.

"That won't happen," she promised him. "It can't."

"If I had understood sooner—"

"You weren't ready before," she said. "Things happen when the time is right, Conrad, and now the time is right for Kaspar to hear Anna's message."

She spoke with apparent confidence, despite a faint flicker of inward doubt that she couldn't quite dispel. Surely Kaspar would stay alive until she reached him? Fate couldn't be so cruel enough to burden Conrad with a lifetime of self-reproach. He was looking at her now with a total trust that went straight to her heart. She prayed that nothing might happen to damage that trust.

She called the airport, and to her overwhelming relief she found that the controllers' slowdown was over. There was a flight leaving for Frankfurt in three hours. She had just enough time to pack up the picture to take along with her. As she was finishing, Conrad said, "Don't forget the package you have to give my grandfather."

"I have it safe," she assured him, pointing to her purse, and smiling because she knew now that he really did understand.

The journey to the airport was fraught with traffic jams. Conrad sat in the back of the taxi, clenching and unclenching his fingers, his face very pale. When they arrived, Laurel went to collect the tickets while he placed a call home. He returned looking tense. "Friederich says he's holding on, but he's so weak that the doctor expects the end at any moment."

On the plane, he held her hand and didn't speak, except once, to say, "Do you have it safe?"

She didn't have to ask what he meant. She took the package from her purse to show him. He took it and looked at it a moment before returning it to her. "And you don't know what's in it?" he asked.

"I've never looked. I don't feel I have any right. But I think—I *know* it's a reaffirmation of her love for him."

He returned it to her. "You were right not to open it. The contents are only for him to see."

Boris was waiting as they hurried out of the airport into the cool night air. "How is he?" Conrad demanded quickly.

"The baron was alive when I left the castle," Boris said.

Conrad squeezed Laurel's hand tightly, and together they got into the back seat. The drive back to Hargen seemed endless. Conrad sat in silence, but despite this, Laurel knew that he hadn't withdrawn from her. His heart and spirit were still hers, but he had no words for the heaviness that burdened him.

At last the castle came in sight, and in another moment they were climbing the steep road. As they neared the top, they could make out the turret where Kaspar lay, and the faint light coming from the arched windows. As the car drew up in the courtyard, they saw Johanna appear in one window and stretch out a hand as if to draw the curtains. "No," Conrad said urgently. "It's not possible."

Laurel felt her heart stop. Had Johanna been drawing the curtains as a sign that it was all over, and they'd come too late? She climbed out and stared upward, but Johanna had seen them and halted the movement. The next moment she'd turned away.

The doctor was waiting for them at the top of the winding stairs. "Thank heavens you came in time," he said. "It can't be much longer."

He stood back to let them pass, but as Conrad was ushering Laurel into the bedroom, he coughed and said, "In view of the baron's extreme weakness, it might be better if only the immediate family..." he fell silent under Conrad's gaze.

"If only one person was allowed to be with him," Conrad said simply, "*she* would be the one."

The room was very quiet. As Laurel entered, she was vaguely aware of Johanna retreating until she was almost flattened against the wall. Friederich was there too, coming swiftly forward to embrace Conrad. But all Laurel's attention was on the frail form on the bed, who lay terribly still with closed eyes, his breath coming faintly. She approached him and stood by the bedside. Conrad went to the other side and leaned over Kaspar, touching him gently.

"Grandfather," he called. "Grandfather, can you hear me?"

After a long moment, the old man opened his eyes. With a great effort, he managed to smile at his grandson. "I've brought someone to see you," Conrad said. He'd meant to explain Laurel's presence, in case the old man should be confused, but suddenly there was an ache in his throat that made it impossible to speak, and he merely pointed to her.

Slowly Kaspar turned his head. As his gaze fell on the young woman by his bedside, her long hair framing her face, his hands made a convulsive movement on the coverlet. But then he grew very still, looking at her in wonder and disbelief.

Laurel showed him the package. "I have brought you something," she said, "from Anna."

The name seemed to rouse him. "Anna..." he whispered. "Anna..."

Laurel moved closer so that she could sit on the bed, and began to open the package. As the paper was removed, a lock of golden hair, tied at one end with ribbon, fell out and lay on the coverlet. It gleamed in the dimly lit room as brightly as the day it had been cut by a young man in love, long ago. Life seemed to return to Kaspar. He reached out a hand, took the hair, and drew it lovingly to his lips. "No other woman ever had hair like yours," he murmured. He lowered his hand and looked directly at Laurel, smiling. "How I loved it, and how you used to tease me. Do you remember that, Anna?"

Conrad made a sudden movement of dismay as he realized what had happened. He looked across at Laurel, with eyes that begged her not to disillusion Kaspar, but realized at once that there was no need. Laurel hadn't even looked at him. She was smiling at Kaspar as she said, "Yes, I remember. You liked me to wear it flowing freely, and I did it up in plaits so that you'd plead with me to take it down." She knew this from listening to Anna, and from the contented look on Kaspar's face, she realized she'd said the right thing.

"And you always did take it down at last," he said. "Or you let me do it. I'd run my fingers through it and call you my Lorelei. And one day—do you remember what I did?"

"You cut a length off," Laurel said.

"Yes, I took it from..." his fingers delicately traced her hairline down as far as her left ear, "just there." He gave her a fond, reminiscent smile. "You said I was bad. You complained that it would show, but it doesn't. You look just the same."

"It grew again," Laurel said, smiling back at him.

"You insisted on taking a lock of my hair, too. I pretended to laugh, but secretly I was glad. That night—" He wavered into silence and for a moment it seemed he might be too weak to go on. But his strength came back and he murmured, "That night, when I was alone, I held your hair against my lips, against my heart, and dreamed of you. You had promised to marry me. Do you remember?"

Laurel leaned closer so that he could see her face. Her features were slightly different from Anna's, but she wasn't afraid of him seeing that. Kaspar was in another world, where only one face existed. "Yes . . . yes, I remember," she assured him.

"But then you went away." His voice grew weary, and there was a note of despair in it. "You promised to belong to me until the end of our lives, and beyond that forever. Why did you leave me, Anna?"

Laurel lifted out the one other thing that the package contained. It was a sealed envelope. With Conrad's eyes on her, she opened it and spread out the page. Kaspar was still watching her out of shadowed eyes, and she realized he'd never be able to read the letter for himself. She reached out a hand to lay it over his, and felt his frail fingers clasp hers. When she was sure her voice was steady, she began to read Anna's last message.

Kaspar, my beloved—for beloved is what you have always been to me, and what you will be until eternity. I love you now as deeply as I did that day I promised to be your wife. I meant that promise, and in my heart I have always been your wife.

I remember everything about the precious time we had together: that little café where I worked as a waitress, and sometimes sang for the customers, and the evening you came in. From the moment I saw you, I sang for you alone.

I remember our days together, when we went walking in the country, and you always filled my arms with wild roses. You said I must carry them when I was your bride. I couldn't believe you were serious, for you were the baron's son, and how could you marry a waitress? But you laughed aside my fears. You couldn't believe that anything could go wrong with a love as perfect as ours.

For a while, it seemed that you were right. Your father appeared to accept me, but I know now that he never did. He let us become engaged, expecting you to tire of me. How little he knew about you, or the great love there was between us.

Three days before what was to have been our wedding day, your father came to see me. He said you would be disgraced by our wedding, that a vulgar little waitress could never be Baroness von Feldstein. He told me all the things you were too generous to tell me— how our friends were turning away from you in disgust because you were shaming your family and your class. I tried to fight him. I said such friends weren't worth having, and that class didn't matter. He replied, "This is the only world he knows, and you will bear a heavy responsibility if you take it from him."

How foolish that sounds now, but in those days such things mattered, and so I came to believe that I could best prove my love for you by going away. I couldn't bear for you to think me false. But I didn't dare see you again. I knew you would try to change my mind, and I wouldn't have the strength to hold out against the look in your eyes and the love in your voice. So I wrote to you, telling you that I still loved you and always would, begging you not to hate me. I gave the letter to your father, and he swore on his honor that he would give it to you.

At the time I never doubted that he would keep his word, but as the years have gone by, I have often wondered if you ever received my letter.

At first, I thought I would die from the loss of you. But I survived and made a life that was not quite empty. In time I had a husband, not a lover like you, but a kind man who gave me a home and a child. I never felt guilty that I still loved you. He had all he wanted from me.

I cut off my hair so that no other man should ever touch it. I had meant to throw it away, but I kept a lock of it. It is unchanged, just as my heart is unchanged, and I send it to you as a pledge. If your heart, too, is the same, you will understand.

Do you remember the day I said I would marry you? We went up to the Lorelei rock, and you said to me, "You are the Lorelei. Now I know she sings a song of love." And we promised ourselves to each other. Later, we found two pictures in a stall in the market. They had been painted from the very spot where we stood, so you bought them, and we took one each, promising to bring them back together on our wedding day. That day never came, but when I left you, I took my picture, to recall the place where we bound our hearts and souls together.

It has stayed with me all these years. It, too, is unaltered, and I know that the rock stands just as it did that day, and the river below glides onward still, reminding me that the years apart that seem so long are but a moment in the eternity of love. The words we said to each other that day have lived in my heart ever since. I shall say them in my last moment. I say them to you now.

Laurel hesitated, then laid down the letter and looked directly at Kaspar. The words she spoke next were Anna's, but they echoed in her own heart, and they sent a message to Conrad that he was only now ready to understand.

"I have loved you," she said. "I shall always love you, until the end of time."

There was a breathless hush in the room when she had finished. Laurel sat immobile, watching Kaspar, moved beyond words by the sight of the disbelieving joy dawning on his face.

"*Liebchen*..." His voice was young and strong. "*Liebchen*, don't cry."

She hadn't known she was weeping until she touched her cheek and found it wet. "If I cry it's because I'm happy," she told him huskily.

"And I, because you have returned to me. They told me you were faithless, but I never believed that... never, because I always knew... You will not leave me again?"

She leaned closer to him, knowing what she must do. She raised Kaspar's hand to lay it tenderly against her cheek, saying in a voice that was suddenly not her own, "No, my beloved. Our parting is over, and now we shall always be together."

Conrad, watching them, held his breath as his grandfather's face changed, and for a moment the young man who'd loved in the springtime of life smiled back, radiant with joy. Then the picture blurred and Conrad turned quickly away, shielding his eyes.

Chapter Twelve

Quietly, Conrad and Laurel crept from the room. There was nothing more for them to do there. He took hold of her hand and didn't let go of it until they reached the drawing room.

There he took her into his arms again. "Thank God," he said fervently. "Thank God we were in time. If we'd been too late, I could never have forgiven myself."

"But we weren't too late," she said. Her voice was full of exultation. Tonight something glorious had happened and the eternal power of it had caught her up, filling her with joy that she wanted to share with the man she loved. It was as though time were seamless, and the love that united her to Conrad was the same love that had brought Kaspar and Anna together after long years apart. She pulled Conrad's head down and laid her lips on his in a silent message that was for his heart alone.

When she released him, Conrad said somberly, "His father never gave him Anna's letter."

"I suppose he was afraid Kaspar would find her and marry her."

"But all those years of suffering—how could he do that to his own son? And he even tried to make him believe Anna was faithless."

"But Kaspar never did believe it," Laurel reminded him. "Remember, he said so."

"I blamed Anna, and all the time the fault lay in my own family. Kaspar told me once that his father was eaten up with pride." Conrad hesitated, then added wryly, "He also said that I was uncomfortably like him."

"He was wrong," Laurel said at once. "The man that could do such a cruel thing could never have come to understand, as you did."

"As you showed me how." He drew her against him, embracing her not with passion, but with relief that he had found his way home at last.

"Lorelei!" The cry from the door made them look up sharply, and a moment later Horst had flung himself at her. "You came back, you came back!" he cried.

"Of course I came back," she said. "How could you think I'd leave you?"

"But Mother told me you'd gone forever."

As he said it, Johanna appeared in the doorway, her face pale and drawn. "It was a mistake," she said desperately. "I must have misunderstood." Her eyes, full of frantic pleading, met Laurel's.

"Of course," Laurel said at once. She smiled at Horst, who was clinging to her. "I left in such a hurry I probably didn't make myself clear."

"But why did you go away?" he persisted.

"It's a long story. I'll tell you another time."

"Are you back to stay for always?" he asked anxiously.

"Yes," Conrad said. "This time she's going to stay for always." He put his hand on Horst's shoulder and looked into his face. "We are going to be married."

He watched anxiously as the implications burst over the child. Suddenly, Horst beamed. "Does that mean I don't ever have to be a baron?" he asked hopefully.

Conrad smiled faintly. "Didn't you like the idea?"

"Not really. I'd much rather be an astronaut."

"Very wise," Conrad said gravely. "That's a much better thing to be."

"It's time you were getting ready for bed," Johanna told the child. "Run along. I'll come up in a moment."

When he'd gone, she closed the door behind him and walked back into the room. Her hands shook and she looked as if she'd been crying. But her manner was dignified as she said to Laurel, "Soon you will be mistress here, and now that you know what I did, you will wish me to leave. I want to tell you that I have already started making my arrangements."

"There's no need for you to leave," Laurel said quickly. She could see the marks of suffering on Johanna's face and she couldn't bring herself to hate her. "This is your home, and Horst's, and you must stay."

"But I destroyed your letter," Johanna cried. "I lied. I never tell lies, and yet—I lied. I did it for Horst, but it was wrong." She gave a choking sob. "I thought it would be easy. I didn't know that I would have to tell another lie, and then another, until I felt so wicked. And then I had to lie to my son . . ." she shuddered.

"He must never know that," Laurel said firmly. "He must always believe it was a misunderstanding."

"You would do that for me?" Johanna asked incredulously. "After what I did to you?" She searched Conrad's face. "But *you* could never forgive me," she insisted, almost challenging him.

"But I can." Conrad laid a kindly hand on her arm. "Let us say no more about it. I owe you more than you will ever know."

Laurel was awoken by a feather-light touch on her lips. She opened her eyes to find Conrad leaning over her. It was dawn and he looked as if he'd dressed in a hurry. "Come with me," he said softly.

She pulled on a robe and followed him out. "Is it your grandfather?" she asked.

"Yes. Don't ask me. Just come."

They made their way through the still-sleeping house and up the stairs of the turret. At the door to Kaspar's room, Conrad stopped and brushed her cheek gently with his fingertips. "Before you go in, I want you to know how eternally grateful I am for all you've done. But for you, this would be a tragedy. As it is—I think I can bring myself to be glad for his sake."

Laurel slipped into the dimly lit room, knowing what she was going to find. Kaspar lay back against his pillows, his eyes closed. One hand was over his heart, and held in it, streaming over his fingers, as bright and glowing as the day it was cut, was a single lock of fair hair. All strain had left him and his face was peaceful and contented, the face of a man who'd found perfect love and fulfillment at last.

"I never saw him look like that in all the years I knew him," Conrad said in a low voice. "And it so nearly didn't happen. Thank you, my darling, for saving me from making a terrible mistake.''

"It's strange," she said, her eyes on Kaspar. "But I can't feel that this is a sad occasion."

"I know. I feel the same, except that I would have liked him to know about our wedding."

Laurel turned and looked earnestly up at him, her arms around his waist. "But don't you see? He doesn't need us."

Conrad nodded. "He only needed one person, and now he has her—because of you." He looked down at his grandfather, who seemed to have fallen into a natural sleep. "When my time comes, I too shall look glad and contented—because of you." He tightened his arms about her. "But, please God, we'll have many years together first."

"Many years," she echoed, "or one year, or one day. It makes no real difference in the end. What we have can never be taken away."

The art expert from Munich paid a discreet visit and studied the paintings side by side. His opinion confirmed all their hopes, and his official evaluation was enough to obtain a loan from the bank before the Friday deadline. With a light heart, Conrad tore up the papers that would have mortgaged the castle.

As a result, to Laurel's bemusement, she found herself the owner of a slice of Feldstein Distillery. When she questioned it, Conrad looked surprised. "It's no more than your right," he said. "You've just given me several hundred thousand pounds. Did you think I was simply going to pocket it and leave you with nothing?"

"I never thought about it," she confessed. "I'm not used to having money."

"And you boasted of being a wealthy woman," he reminded her with a smile.

"I didn't know how rich I really was," she said, with a caress that told him her real meaning.

He had a sudden anxious thought. "They wouldn't mind us risking their pictures, would they?"

Laurel shook her head. "Anna would have been proud to help save Kaspar's home, especially after his father had told her she wasn't good enough for him. How strange, the way things work out!"

"Like a circle that ends where it begins," he mused. "Their ending, our beginning... and their beginning."

She smiled. "I wondered if you'd see that."

"I'm seeing a great many things these days that I never dreamed of before. I feel as if I've been walking through the world, blind, but now the darkness has gone."

A month later, they married in the private chapel of Feldstein Castle, the same chapel where the wedding of Kaspar and Anna should have taken place. The ceremony was the quietest possible, and the only guests were some von Feldstein cousins, and Stefan, the customs officer, who was best man.

The plaster cast had been removed from Laurel's ankle at last, and she was determined to be married without even a cane. Some determined practice got her strength back, and on her wedding day there was no hesitation in her step as she walked down the aisle on Friederich's arm. She was breathtaking in a white silk dress, cut on deliberately simple lines, and carrying a bouquet of wild roses.

Laurel barely noticed her surroundings. She had eyes only for the man whose love filled her whole existence. And from his expression as he saw her walking toward him, she knew that for him, too, nothing mattered but the two of them, and the promises they would make to each other—promises of love for life and beyond.

Horst behaved angelically during the service, but then apparently decided that enough was enough, and enlivened the wedding breakfast by making a dramatic entrance in his monster costume. Some of the older cousins were inclined to be shocked, but Laurel laughed and said a wedding needed a mischievous child to make it complete. A buzz went around the family that the new baroness would do very well.

Laurel and Conrad had decided to leave the honeymoon until later. All they needed now was to be alone together, and that night, when the guests had gone and the house was finally quiet, they had their wish.

Conrad closed the door of his bedroom and locked it with a sigh of relief. Then he turned to look at her standing in the light from the one lamp, softly radiant in her white wedding dress, adorned only by his gift of pearls. He opened his arms and she went into them, raising her face for his kiss.

He kissed her slowly, as though trying to reassure himself that all this was real, and she wouldn't vanish from his arms. Then his embrace tightened with the overwhelming realization that she was here and she belonged to him. His lips began to caress hers more urgently, pleading and demanding until she opened her mouth with a sigh.

She could feel Conrad's fingers at the fastening of her dress. With her help he got it free and the garment slid with a whisper to the floor. He lifted her out of it and laid her on the bed, worshipping her with his eyes. She began to undress him, pulling his shirt off and running her fingers deliciously through the hair of his chest, sensing the eager pulsing of desire through his body. Her own senses leaped to answer it. She was aflame with passion and adoration, wanting to be one with him, wanting to make their love complete. She seemed to have been waiting all her life for this moment and now it had come.

He traced her curves lovingly, holding his breath with disbelief at the revelation of so much beauty. His fingers lingered over the swell of her breasts, the roundness of her hips and her long, elegant legs. The real beauty, as he knew when he looked into her eyes, was not in her body but in her heart, full of love for him. And at that realization, he could contain himself no longer. He spoke her name urgently, and at her answer, he moved over her and claimed his greatest joy.

Laurel lay in his arms, moving to the rhythm of love fulfilled, feeling the bonds that linked her to this man grow stronger with every sensitive caress, every passionate whisper. When their moment came, she surrendered with ecstasy, giving herself freely, holding nothing back, and knew that it was the same with him.

Gradually, the thunder of their hearts subsided and they lay curled in each others arms, fulfilled and content. Laurel kissed him and rose from the bed, drawing a silk robe about her. Conrad's eyes never left her as she went to the window overlooking the gorge, and after a moment she heard him behind her. He enfolded her in his arms and rested his head against hers as they looked out at the night and the stars. The brilliant moon cast a shimmering glow over the proud peak of the rock, and around it flowed soft echoing sounds that danced from bank to bank before swirling down the river and onward to eternity.

"Can you hear her singing?" Conrad murmured.

In answer, she pressed herself closer to her husband and they stood together in harmonious silence, listening to the song of the Lorelei. Now they could hear it clearly for the first time, and it was a song of true love.

* * * * *

WRITTEN IN THE STARS

**Star-crossed lovers?
Or a match made in heaven?**

Why are some heroes strong and silent ... and others charming and cheerful? The answer is WRITTEN IN THE STARS!

Coming each month in 1991, Silhouette Romance presents you with a special love story written by one of your favorite authors—highlighting the hero's astrological sign! From January's sensible Capricorn to December's disarming Sagittarius, you'll meet a dozen dazzling and distinct heroes.

Twelve heavenly heroes ... twelve wonderful Silhouette Romances destined to delight you. Look for one WRITTEN IN THE STARS title every month throughout 1991—only from Silhouette Romance.

STAR

Silhouette Books®

ARE YOU A ROMANCE READER WITH OPINIONS?

Openings are currently available for participation in the 1990-1991 Romance Reader Panel. We are looking for new participants from all regions of the country and from all age ranges.

If selected, you will be polled once a month by mail to comment on new books you have recently purchased, and may occasionally be asked for more in-depth comments. Individual responses will remain confidential and all postage will be prepaid.

Regular purchasers of one favorite series, as well as those who sample a variety of lines each month, are needed, so fill out and return this application today for more detailed information.

1. Please indicate the romance series you purchase from regularly at retail outlets.

Harlequin	Silhouette	
1. ☐ Romance	6. ☐ Romance	10. ☐ Bantam Loveswept
2. ☐ Presents	7. ☐ Special Edition	11. ☐ Other _____
3. ☐ American Romance	8. ☐ Intimate Moments	
4. ☐ Temptation	9. ☐ Desire	
5. ☐ Superromance		

2. Number of romance paperbacks you purchase new in an average month:

   12.1 ☐ 1 to 4   .2 ☐ 5 to 10   .3 ☐ 11 to 15   .4 ☐ 16+

3. Do you currently buy romance   13.1 ☐ yes   .2 ☐ no
   series through direct mail?

   If yes, please indicate series: _____
                                                    (14,15)   (16,17)

4. Date of birth: _____ / _____ / _____
                  (Month)   (Day)   (Year)
                   18,19   20,21   22,23

5. Please print:
   Name: _____
   Address: _____
   City: _____ State: _____ Zip: _____
   Telephone No. (optional): (_____) _____

MAIL TO: Attention: Romance Reader Panel
         Consumer Opinion Center
         P.O. Box 1395
         Buffalo, NY 14240-9961   ☐☐☐☐☐☐☐☐☐☐☐☐

                              Office Use Only   SRDK

OFFICIAL SWEEPSTAKES
ENTRY FORM

Complete and return this Entry Form immediately—the more Entry Forms you submit, the better your chances of winning!
- Entry Forms must be received by **December 31, 1990**
- A random draw will take place on **January 29, 1991**
- Trip must be taken by **December 31, 1991**

3-SR-3-SW

YES, I want to win a PASSPORT TO ROMANCE vacation for two! I understand the prize includes round-trip air fare, accommodation and a daily spending allowance.

Name_____

Address_____

City_____ State_____ Zip_____

Telephone Number_____ Age_____

Return entries to: **PASSPORT TO ROMANCE**, P.O. Box 9056, Buffalo, NY 14269-9056

© 1990 Harlequin Enterprises Limited

COUPON BOOKLET/OFFER CERTIFICATE

Item	LEVEL ONE Booklet 1	LEVEL TWO Booklet 1 & 2	LEVEL THREE Booklet 1, 2 & 3	LEVEL FOUR Booklet 1, 2, 3 & 4
Booklet 1 = $100+	$100+	$100+	$100+	$100+
Booklet 2 = $200+		$200+	$200+	$200+
Booklet 3 = $300+			$300+	$300+
Booklet 4 = $400+	____	____	____	$400+
Approximate Total Value of Savings	$100+	$300+	$600+	$1,000+
# of Proofs of Purchase Required	4	6	12	18
Check One	____	____	____	____

Name_____

Address_____

City_____ State_____ Zip_____

Return Offer Certificates to: **PASSPORT TO ROMANCE**, P.O. Box 9057, Buffalo, NY 14269-9057

Requests must be postmarked by **January 25, 1991**

- ✂ - - - - - - - - - -

ONE PROOF OF PURCHASE

3-SR-3

To collect your free coupon booklet you must include the necessary number of proofs-of-purchase with a properly completed Offer Certificate

© 1990 Harlequin Enterprises Limited

See previous page for details

PASSPORT TO ROMANCE
SWEEPSTAKES RULES

1. **HOW TO ENTER:** To enter, you must be the age of majority and complete the official entry form, or print your name, address, telephone number and age on a plain piece of paper and mail to: Passport to Romance, P.O. Box 9056, Buffalo, NY 14269-9056. No mechanically reproduced entries accepted.

2. All entries must be received by the CONTEST CLOSING DATE, DECEMBER 31, 1990 TO BE ELIGIBLE.

3. **THE PRIZES:** There will be ten (10) Grand Prizes awarded, each consisting of a choice of a trip for two people from the following list:
   - i) London, England (approximate retail value $5,050 U.S.)
   - ii) England, Wales and Scotland (approximate retail value $6,400 U.S.)
   - iii) Carribean Cruise (approximate retail value $7,300 U.S.)
   - iv) Hawaii (approximate retail value $9,550 U.S.)
   - v) Greek Island Cruise in the Mediterranean (approximate retail value $12,250 U.S.)
   - vi) France (approximate retail value $7,300 U.S.)

4. Any winner may choose to receive any trip or a cash alternative prize of $5,000.00 U.S. in lieu of the trip.

5. **GENERAL RULES:** Odds of winning depend on number of entries received.

6. A random draw will be made by Nielsen Promotion Services, an independent judging organization, on January 29, 1991, in Buffalo, NY, at 11:30 a.m. from all eligible entries received on or before the Contest Closing Date.

7. Any Canadian entrants who are selected must correctly answer a time-limited, mathematical skill-testing question in order to win.

8. Full contest rules may be obtained by sending a stamped, self-addressed envelope to: "Passport to Romance Rules Request", P.O. Box 9998, Saint John, New Brunswick, Canada E2L 4N4.

9. Quebec residents may submit any litigation respecting the conduct and awarding of a prize in this contest to the Régie des loteries et courses du Québec.

10. Payment of taxes other than air and hotel taxes is the sole responsibility of the winner.

11. Void where prohibited by law

COUPON BOOKLET OFFER TERMS

To receive your Free travel-savings coupon booklets, complete the mail-in Offer Certificate on the preceeding page, including the necessary number of proofs-of-purchase, and mail to: Passport to Romance, P.O. Box 9057, Buffalo, NY 14269-9057. The coupon booklets include savings on travel-related products such as car rentals, hotels, cruises, flowers and restaurants. Some restrictions apply. The offer is available in the United States and Canada. Requests must be postmarked by January 25, 1991. Only proofs-of-purchase from specially marked "Passport to Romance" Harlequin® or Silhouette® books will be accepted. The offer certificate must accompany your request and may not be reproduced in any manner. Offer void where prohibited or restricted by law. LIMIT FOUR COUPON BOOKLETS PER NAME, FAMILY, GROUP, ORGANIZATION OR ADDRESS. Please allow up to 8 weeks after receipt of order for shipment. Enter quickly as quantities are limited. Unfulfilled mail-in offer requests will receive free Harlequin® or Silhouette® books (not previously available in retail stores), in quantities equal to the number of proofs-of-purchase required for Levels One to Four, as applicable.